BEFORE
OUREYES

Other books by the author

A Boy's Best Friend (with Catherine Hopkins)
Letting In The Night
Mrs. Cooper's Boardinghouse

BEFORE OUREYES

A NOVEL

JOAN ALDEN

author of *Letting in the Night*

Firebrand
Books
Ithaca, New York

Book design by Betsy Bayley
Cover design and photograph by Catherine Hopkins
Typesetting by Bets Ltd.

Printed in the United States on acid-free paper by McNaughton & Gunn

Library of Congress Cataloging-in-Publication Data

Alden, Joan.
   Before our eyes : a novel / by Joan Alden.
      p.   cm.
      ISBN 1-56341-034-6 (alk. paper). — ISBN 1-56341-033-8 (pbk. : alk. paper)
      1. Adult children of alcoholics—United States—Fiction.
   2. Family—United States—Fiction.   3. Women—United States-Fiction.   I. Title.
   PS3562.I496B4   1993
813'.54—dc20
                                                          93-30089
                                                              CIP

To Lynn Waters Reeser

one

I drive home
on the Long Island
Expressway headed east. A
day of rain followed by drizzle has
melted away most of the snow New York got
earlier in the week, leaving those small, nearly black piles
at the sides of the roads. Then I sit in the car in the drive and stare
at the large red brick and brown-shingled house Jeff and I grew up
in. I haven't been here in nearly six months.

Everything looks the same from the outside, except the awnings aren't up. Dad takes them down each fall. When asked my first day of school to give my address, I said my house had green-and-white striped awnings.

As the car windows steam up, the big house before me seems more and more unreal. I feel like I'm in a dream, and maybe I wish I were. I stay in the car for close to a half hour, working up the courage to go in. Then I take a deep breath and get out of the car with my suitcase and camera bag.

The front door is open, and when I call out, Jeff's nurse steps into the hallway. "I'm home," I say, but don't follow her into what was once the dining room and is now Jeff's room. Instead I head up the stairs. I want to settle in a bit before I have to be with anyone.

After setting my suitcase and camera bag down inside the door to my room, I go to Jeff's old room. It is exactly as he left it fourteen years ago. The only thing missing is his Pentax camera, which I took, and his enlarger, timer, and trays from his bathroom. The windows and furnishings are dusty. I was the only one who spent any time here after Jeff's accident, preferring this room to the dining room: this is where my brother was, not lying in the hospital bed downstairs.

I used to stretch out on the twin bed and look through Jeff's photography books, or stare at the solar system he had painted on the ceiling, or sit at the desk and go through his stack of baseball cards, or walk around the room examining every detail of Jeff's photos hanging on the bedroom walls. One is of a dog and a toddler on the beach. The dog is shaking water from his fur, and the toddler is falling backward as if by the spray of water. Another is of me doing a cartwheel in our backyard. These pictures were taken when Jeff was eight and nine years old and, like Lartigue's early photos, show sensitivity and whimsy as well as promise. The other photos in the room are landscapes: a birch at the edge of a lake, a tide pool, a marsh, and the Sound on a stormy day. More than beautiful photographs, they are haunting. I am sure I will never be the photographer Jeff would have been. It seems as likely to me that he would have become a better marine architect than Dad because of his sense of design, and a better storyteller than Mom because of his willingness to play the fool. The best of us was lost.

There are two other bedrooms on the second floor. The larger, with a fireplace, is where my folks once slept and where I was born. The other is where Mom slept after the accident. She told me she moved there because she didn't want to wake my father when she got up in the middle of the night to check on Jeff. The door to Mom's old room is locked. I wonder why, and will look for the key later.

I return to my room and open the closetlike door to the back stairs which climb from the kitchen below to the third floor where Dad's studio is. I don't go up to look at it. Instead, I walk over to my dresser. On top of it sits a leather box with my initials stamped on the front in gold leaf. It was a gift from my dad many Christmases ago. I never had enough jewelry to require a jewelry box so I filled it with small shells and pieces of colored glass I collected from the beach. I open the box. Nothing at all lies on the worn satin.

Before going downstairs I peek into the sewing room at the back of the house. On the floor, beside a chaise, is a round basket where Mom kept her thread. I bend down and lift off the lid. The basket is full of colorful spools neatly arranged in concentric circles. It is exactly as it was the last time I looked. It pleases me to think that no one but me ever opens this basket.

On my way back down to the library, I pass the door to the trunk room under the stairway. At one time there was an old steamer trunk in there full of shoes belonging to Dad. He tired of shoes long before they wore out but couldn't bear to part with them. While most kids played doctor and nurse, or cowboys and Indians, Jeff and I played shoe salesman and customer. We'd haul out every blessed shoe and line them up in the hallway. It nearly drove Mom nuts. She complained we cut off her access to the library, but I always suspected it was Dad's extravagance that truly annoyed her. To Mom, having one of anything was plenty. There was a time in her life before she married Dad when she couldn't afford more than that, and her desires never increased with her means. In the sixth grade I envied a classmate for, among other things, a red cardigan she wore. When I requested a sweater like hers for my birthday, Mom asked me what was wrong with the blue sweater I already had.

The library of our house opens onto a porch, with battleship gray floorboards, which extends all along the back and one side of the house. Beyond it is a lawn ending at a cliff wall, and beyond that is Long Island Sound. To the east lies Setauket Beach, where I spent many summer days.

Looking out in that direction I recall an incident from my childhood. A neighbor told Mom that she had seen me skinny-dipping in the Sound. Afraid I would get in trouble for that, Jeff said he was the one the woman had seen, not me, and although Jeff was never a very good liar, Mom let it pass. I didn't expect her to disapprove since she went skinny-dipping at the lake.

I step over to a section of bookshelves, pull out a special book, and the section opens as a door. I was seven years old when I discovered this entrance to the dining room and bragged to all my friends that there were secret passages in my house.

Jeff is in his sleep phase, so I don't feel compelled to say something to him in front of the nurse. She asks me if I'd like to be alone with my brother. I nod yes, but that's because I don't want to have to put on a performance. Although I feel correct in rejecting this Jeff, I don't trust that others would understand and I'm not confident enough to be comfortable with that.

My brother has been in a persistent vegetative state for fourteen years, a year longer than his life before the boat accident. His body is reasonably healthy, although he is unnaturally smooth and soft, his feet and hands are turned in, and his neck is hyperextended. He can breathe on his own, and since he has a gag reflex, theoretically he can eat. But it is difficult to place food back far enough on his tongue to make him swallow, so he has a nasogastric feeding tube instead. He has periods of wakefulness and periods of sleep. When Jeff is awake his eyes are open and wander, not following people or objects in a meaningful way.

Jeff cannot and will not ever again be able to see, hear, speak, respond, think, or feel on even the most rudimentary level. All that remains is a living body that used to be the living body of a person. It is not my brother. To me it is not even a reminder of my brother. It is the body of a man, not a boy. I am bothered by the sight and smell of this Jeff who lies motionless in bed, his legs so thin they barely make a ridge under the bed covers, his hands crippled by muscle contractions, his head thrust back unnaturally, and the room, furnishings, and Jeff giving off a stale odor. I cannot bring myself to speak to Jeff here. We talk in his room upstairs.

I reach out and touch Jeff's hand. He is warm, and that confuses me. Sometimes I have to struggle not to be confused into thinking Jeff is alive.

Hanging on the wall in this room is a photograph of a Class J sloop that raced for the America's Cup in 1937. My dad is one of the crew on board. Next to that photograph is one of the Nelrud, a fifty-foot schooner designed by Dad. My family and I sailed it down to the Bahamas the summer I was ten years old. Incredibly, I don't remember anything of the trip. Beside these two photos is a photo by Jeff's favorite photographer. It is Minor White's *Ocean—Schoodic Point, Maine 1968*, which Dad bought for Jeff on what would have been Jeff's fourteenth birthday. The photo is a picture of cliff rock split by the force of the water. I think of this as a metaphor for my broken brother.

Other photos of our family hang on the walls in the room—almost all of them taken by Jeff. He always had his camera at family gatherings. One by one I look at each, stopping finally at a picture of Jeff standing on the dock of the cabin in Connecticut. He is twelve years old in the photo. It was shot the summer before his boat accident. Beside that photo is one of Mom and Dad at a Christmas party. Dad is slouched against Mom and has a drink in his hand.

I walk out of the dining room and into the kitchen. Jeff's nurse is there, and she tells me she is going to give Jeff a feeding, then leave for the night. I pour myself a cup of coffee and sit down at the kitchen table, glancing at the clock as I do. I have an hour to get ready.

Suddenly I'm back in junior high. I've just come in from school and set my books down on the kitchen table. There's a note from Mom, telling me that she and Dad won't be home for dinner; I should make the nurse and myself soup and sandwiches.

Dad would come home alone later that night and tell me that Mom had breast cancer, that her right breast would have to be removed. I found him drunk at Jeff's side at two in the morning. He said he couldn't face life without my mother. I didn't like hearing that. I wanted to be told that Mom would be all right. I wanted to be told that no matter what happened I would be all right. I knew if it were Dad taking care of me, I would not be. Mom was never drunk and unable to cope. Mom could make things right no matter how wrong they got. She had more surprises up her sleeves than a magician, knew all the ballet positions without ever taking dance lessons, and could change her voice with each character in a story as she read aloud.

I glance up at the clock again. I have just enough time to dress.

A dozen or so people are at the funeral home when I arrive. Most are colleagues of Dad's. Chris and Ted Rooney from the yacht club are also present, and Bob Benson, a neighbor. Of all the people I would have liked to see it's Meg, Bob's wife, who for some reason isn't with him. The minister introduces himself to me. He's the new pastor at the Presbyterian church in town where my family belongs, where we went on Christmas and Easter.

Before the service begins I approach Dad's casket. It is closed. Dad left no instructions, so I decided there would not be a church service or viewing of Dad's body, and after this informal service he would be cremated and his ashes buried in the town cemetery.

The pastor has an easy voice to listen to—it's conversational, not preachy. But he knows practically nothing about my father, so his message is general and the service blessedly short. Afterward, Bob Benson comes up to me to explain that Meg is sick with the flu and is sorry she couldn't make it. I promise to call her the next day but know that I won't.

Chris and Ted have something for me and follow me home. Ted carries a basket of fruit to the kitchen while Chris and I visit in the hallway. I ask her if she wants to see Jeff before she leaves but don't accompany her when she steps into the dining room.

Chris and Ted were Dad's drinking buddies—Chris as much as Ted. When I was young I blamed them for Dad's behavior because whenever they were guests in our house Dad got sloshed.

Chris returns to Ted and me in the hall and says, "I guess you'll be coming home now that your dad's gone."

I shake my head and say, "I'm going to sell it."

"What about Jeff?" Chris asks.

I don't respond. It's an awkward moment.

Ted asks me if I'm going to be all right.

I answer, "Yes."

"We could stay," Chris offers, "until the nurse returns."

I don't tell them the nurse won't be returning. "I'm fine alone," I say. "I can take care of Jeff."

"Call us if you need anything," Ted says on his way out.

I don't dislike Chris or Ted, and I no longer need to make them scapegoats. They're decent folk and were loyal friends to my father, but they would not be friends of mine except for Dad.

I go to Jeff when they leave. He's awake, his eyes wandering about the room as I wash him and change his diaper. Once I have him settled on his side, I walk through the library to the porch and then outside.

It is pitch dark and cold. I walk down to the cliff wall, then back to the house, and huddle under a heavy blanket on the porch swing. Even in the winter months I would come out here after school, lie perfectly still, and watch the birds at the feeder. Lying in the dark, I imagine I'm at my window in the city, watching the neighbor's kids playing trampoline on an old mattress at the curb. Years ago I took a series of photos of them and sold one to *LIFE*. That success impressed Dad. Thoughts of him bring me back to the porch. The load I have decided to carry suddenly feels too heavy, and I wish Mom were here to help me. It isn't wrong that this should fall upon me, since I argued for it, but I imagined myself more capable and courageous than I am.

The screen door swings open and Jeff leaps out onto the porch wearing only his pajama bottoms.

"Look, Bernie, Mom gave me a flat-top!"

I glance up from my book to see that Jeff no longer has sideburns, that the hair on top of his head is less than a half-inch long. "I never knew you had such big ears," I say, and Jeff gets a worried look on his face. He thought he looked great, but now, because of me, he's not sure. His big sister has the power to shake his confidence.

As Jeff's smile fades, his form does also. Mom appears in his place on the porch with two cups of hot chocolate. She sits down on the swing beside me and hands me one of the cups.

"He lost," she says.

"We knew he would," I answer.

"Why don't you come in?"

"Because Dad will gloat."

"You weren't the one to vote for McGovern."

"I would have if I was old enough. This is the most depressing night of my life," I say.

"Lucky for you," Mom says, and as quickly as she disappears into the house, Dad appears on the porch with his shirt sleeves rolled up above his elbows.

"Come on in, Bern, and see your brother."

"But it's so nice out here."

"Come be with the family. We need you."

"Why?"

"Be a sport, Bern."

"I don't want to be a sport."

"Yes, you do," he says, and I get up and follow him in.

I lay the blanket I carried in from the porch on the library sofa, turn off the light in Jeff's room, and head upstairs.

Halfway up I see Gillian coming down toward me. She stops on the step above me and says she's sorry I'm leaving, knowing it's because of her I've changed my plans. I nod my head, chagrinned. Her genuineness makes me feel shoddy, but it is because she is so appealing that I am frightened.

At the top of the stairs the door to the sewing room is open and I can see Mom lying on the chaise with Jeff on her lap and me on the floor beside them, playing with the spools of thread.

Minutes later I am in bed unable to sleep. I imagine I hear Dad overhead, working in his studio. I am fighting the silence.

two

four years earlier

Jeff kept
Mom and Dad an-
chored. Whenever I was
lonely or bored I could go home for a
day or two. One of them was always there.
Rarely did I call ahead of time. I'd simply appear, seek-
ing out their company for my own sake. Then, once my confidence
was restored, I'd take off for the day with my camera. Another daughter might have helped more with Jeff. I'm sure Jeff would have helped
more with me had the tables been turned. Although Mom never
made me feel I should do more, I felt guilty for being the whole one,
and for not being more helpful.

Maybe that was why I didn't ask her why she wanted me to
come home for a few days. Would she have coaxed me to if I hadn't
said yes immediately? Somehow I feel she might have.

I can see Mom on the platform, tall and suntanned in faded
blue shorts, wearing those paint-speckled loafers that are as old as
the hills. She sees me get off the train and waves, then gives me a
great hug when I reach her.

Mom takes my camera bag, and we head for the car. I've always
thought Citroens were ugly, but Mom's has grown on me. I throw
my duffel bag onto the backseat and hop into the front.

"Hot in the City?" Mom asks, as she hands over my camera bag.

"It can go in the back," I say. Mom is careful with my cameras. She has noticed I treat them differently than I do my other possessions. "God awful," I answer, "but I've been in California most of July."

Mom weaves in and out of traffic. I don't expect her to pick up on what I've said because she's focused on her driving. Mom's single-mindedness made it nearly impossible to break her concentration. As small children, Jeff and I could interrupt Dad at work in his studio but never Mom if she was into one of her projects. It was as though she didn't see or hear us. Dad didn't seem to mind being interrupted. I liked that about him. I inherited my mother's raptness, and consequently understood the complaints about me—that I was difficult to reach at times.

I ask Mom why we're stopping at the grocery, and she says we need ice for the cabin.

"Are we going up there?" I ask.

"You want to, don't you?"

"Dad, too?" I ask, knowing better.

The Citroen settles down like a barber chair. Mom shakes her head. I would have been surprised if she had indicated otherwise. Dad hasn't returned to the cabin since Jeff's accident.

Mom isn't gone more than a few minutes. She puts the bag of ice in the trunk and, getting into the car, tosses me a Baby Ruth.

"How long have you got?" she asks me, as she starts up the motor.

"I have some printing to do, but not much else. I guess I could stay a week."

"We'll spend tomorrow and Sunday up there and then come home so you can visit with your dad. How's that?"

"Only a couple days?" I say.

"More?"

"How about five up there and two at home?" I ask.

"Your dad might feel cheated—no, that's good," Mom says.

We pull around the side of the house.

"Is Dad home?" I ask.

"Sure."

"Where is he?" I say, once we're inside.

"Upstairs," Mom answers.

It isn't like Dad not to be waiting for me. "Did he know you were picking me up?" I ask.

"Go up and get him," Mom says.

If Mom had been upstairs instead of Dad, I would have done exactly that.

After putting the ice in the freezer, Mom motions for me to follow her out to the garden. She loads me up with cucumbers and carries fresh tomatoes back to the house. While she fixes supper, I sit at the kitchen table and talk to her. I ask how she's been, hoping she'll say what her invitation home is about, and she answers she's fine but looks preoccupied by something.

Dad wanted others to share in his burdens and would announce every ache and pain he had. Mom never told anyone when she wasn't feeling well or when she was unhappy. I admired Mom's strength. She needed little encouragement or support in facing her life, a characteristic which I, perhaps too easily, rationalized was because her childhood had not been privileged like my father's—she had been forced to be resourceful and self-reliant. But maybe she and Dad had been born with their natures.

I wanted a man like my mother, and they were hard to find. I thought I had found one, but he was as irresponsible as he was independent, wanting to come and go at will, not wanting me or anyone to expect anything from him.

I volunteer that I took pictures in Sonoma, California for *East-West* magazine, and Mom asks what kind.

"It's a piece on organically grown grapes."

"Not your usual," Mom says. My usual are portraits of people doing ordinary things.

"No, but an inexpensive way to get out to California."

"Did you see anyone?" Mom asks.

"I shouldn't have," I answer, "but I thought I was over him." I could admit this to Mom because she never told me there was something wrong with me for loving a man who couldn't make a commitment.

Dad had no idea about my romantic life unless Mom told him things, and if she did, he never asked me about men.

I once lived with a man for two months before he drove me nuts with his demand for attention. Paul agreed to move into my small apartment because I wouldn't think of leaving my darkroom, then complained whenever I spent time in it. When he began to refer to my camera as my true love, I sent him packing. "You aren't forgetting True Love?" he'd ask as we started out the door to go somewhere. Sometime later I realized Paul was my father and I was surprised at myself for choosing such a man.

Because Mark was also a photographer he understood that particular compulsion and was only too happy to do his thing while I was doing mine. Mark never moved in, but he did camp with me when he was in town. Mark lived in Berkeley and traveled all over the world. We were introduced by a former teacher at Cooper Union.

"It will probably take someone else," Mom says, instead of, "You ought to get over Mark."

I glance at the door to the hall several times as I watch Mom get dinner ready, expecting Dad to join us any moment. When he doesn't, Mom goes upstairs to tell him dinner's on the table.

Mom and I are both seated when Dad shuffles into the kitchen with a drink. He looks especially grim. I'm ready for it when he opens his mouth.

"No," I answer, "I haven't been in to see Jeff. Mom and I were visiting."

"Well, has anybody thought about him?" Dad asks, looking to Mom.

"I took care of Jeff before I left to pick up Bern."

"How many hours ago was that?" he asks, sounding unusually sharp. Dad is sullen, not argumentative, when he drinks.

"He'll be fine until we finish," Mom says, but Dad isn't satisfied with that. He gets up from the table and leaves the room. A minute later we hear a Chopin nocturne playing in the dining room. Mom gets up and takes Dad's dinner in to him, then returns to me in the kitchen.

"That's it?" I say. "That's all I get? *Have you seen your brother yet?*"

Mom doesn't defend Dad nor explain to me what's going on. Something is going on, I know that. It's true that when I was living at home the first thing Dad would say to me when I came in was have you seen your brother. But I haven't visited in several months, haven't lived here for many years, and I expected Dad to show some interest in me.

When I was a teenager I would often lie and say, yes, I'd been in to see Jeff. Who was going to tell on me? Later, I expressed my belief that Jeff was not there and I felt stupid saying hello to him and telling him about my day. Dad argued I didn't know where Jeff was, and if Jeff were aware, he would be deeply hurt by my rejection. The doctors had told us Jeff was not aware, but in doubting the doctor's judgment Dad managed to make me doubt my motives.

"I guess you think it shouldn't bother me that Dad's more interested in Jeff," I say to Mom. She doesn't answer. "What's going on?" I ask her.

"If you can wait until tomorrow it would be better," she says, sounding serious. Maybe I don't want to know what's wrong.

We eat in silence. When Mom senses my imagination is running wild she says, "It isn't as awful as that."

After dinner I do the dishes. Mom goes out on the porch where Dad is. From where I'm standing, drying dishes, I can see Dad on the swing and Mom in one of the chairs, but I can't hear either of them.

When the dishes are put away I go into the library and look out on the porch. Mom and Dad are gone. I walk into the dining room.

The room smells of shaving cream. Why did Dad shave Jeff? Mom does that in the morning. Maybe he wanted to make it look like she had neglected him. I wonder if Dad was hurt that I didn't run up to see him when I came home and then transferred his feeling slighted onto Jeff.

In the morning, I put on a pair of shorts and tennis shoes and pack a change of clothes to take to the cabin. Downstairs I approach Mom in the dining room. She's giving Jeff a bath. This is her second session with him today. At eight o'clock she changes his diaper, then does a half hour of range of motion exercises and an hour of feeding followed by teeth cleaning—done with a lemon and glycerin swab on a stick. At ten she bathes and shaves Jeff, then changes his diaper and his position in bed. At noon a visiting nurse changes Jeff's diaper, feeds him, and cleans his mouth. At two o'clock the nurse does the range of motion exercises, changes Jeff's diaper and bed position, and leaves. At four Mom changes Jeff's diaper, feeds him, and cleans his mouth. At six o'clock Dad is usually home and he changes Jeff's diaper and does the range of motion exercises. At eight Dad feeds Jeff for the last time and cleans his mouth. And at ten o'clock Jeff's diaper is changed.

When I was a teenager I wasn't permitted to watch as Jeff was bathed. Now that I'm a grown woman it is apparently all right that I see him naked. Jeff is fair-skinned and soft. Although his bones grew in length and density as he aged, Jeff never got any muscle tone or bulk.

Mom talks to Jeff lovingly while she washes him. In this helpless state Jeff garners more attention and affection than he did, or I do, in the full swing of life. I don't resent this anymore. If I have any resentment it is because Mom and Dad seem to get something out of caring for Jeff's body and I don't.

Mom tells me Dad's in the kitchen, fixing breakfast, and I go to him. He gives me a good morning hug and asks me if I want French toast. I never refuse French toast. This makes up for last night, I tell myself—have told myself all my life, not just wanting to believe everything is back to normal because Dad is, but that he will stay this way.

But everything is not back to normal. Mom and Dad aren't speaking to one another. Over breakfast they speak to me and through me to one another. I hate this. It is the one time Mom seems childish to me.

As soon as I finish my breakfast Mom says we have to go. Twice she has said we have to hurry if we're going to make the eleven o'clock ferry.

"See you on Wednesday!" I holler out the car window to Dad as we leave. He is standing in the driveway in his robe and slippers, waving to me. When he goes into the house he will pour himself a scotch, put on a tape, and sit with Jeff. I don't know for how long, but it isn't difficult to imagine Dad sitting with Jeff all day. The tragedy of his life seems also to be his solace.

On our way to Port Jefferson, Mom and I pass some kids on skateboards. They're backlit and make interesting silhouettes. I would love to stop and take a picture of them, but Mom has reservations for the eleven o'clock ferry. To Mark, a ferry reservation would be less important than catching a fleeting moment. Good photographers must live in the moment. It's a dilemma for me because I'm also a planner. I like the sense of security I give myself by making appointments with a future. Mark lives too carelessly in the moment for me, but that is also what I find exciting about being with him.

Mom parks the car on the ferry, and we get out for the crossing to Bridgeport. I take my Leica with me and shoot several pictures of a young mother on deck. The baby in her arms cries the entire journey across the Sound.

Once off the ferry, Mom and I head northeast toward Konold Pond, then pass Lake Dawson and Lake Watrous before we see signs for Lake Lydia.

Mom built the one-room log cabin with the help of a local man and his son. The pine trees which front the cabin nearly hide it from view. There's no electricity, gas, or running water. Cooking is done on ironware in the fireplace or on a grill outside. There's an ice chest for refrigeration, which keeps things cool, not cold, an outdoor pump, and an outhouse. The floor of the cabin is pine, painted dark green. Bathing suits, towels, and pajamas hang from wooden pegs on the walls. There are four chairs and a card table, a couch, a rocker, two wall bunks, and a loft bed. At the back of the cabin there's a boardwalk to a dock where a row boat is tied up.

I set my things down on one of the bunks, and Mom fills the ice chest with ice and groceries. Then I open the cabin windows as Mom sweeps out the cabin. Afterward we change into our swimsuits.

Mom has small breasts, so those who don't know would probably not notice that one is missing. She never wears a bra and therefore no falsie to compensate for her loss. If Mom were missing a leg, she'd probably have a peg instead of a prosthesis.

As usual, she races down the dock and dives right into the lake. I can't do that. I have to stick a toe in and test the water first.

"Come on in!" she hollers. "It's not cold."

"Like hell it's not," I answer.

"Just dive in, Bern."

Why does she always do this?

"Don't be a dope," she says.

"Go to hell," I answer under my breath.

I watch Mom cut through the water as though she had a motor attached to her butt. When she gets about a third of the way across the lake and all I can see is her head bobbing, I ease my way off the dock into the water. It's so cold it takes my breath away.

"Nice, isn't it?" Mom says on her return.

"If you're a polar bear," I answer and heave myself up on the dock to stretch out in the sun. The boards warm my backside, and I relax and enjoy the smell of the sunbaked pine.

"Oooo, doesn't this feel good," Mom says, lying down beside me on the dock.

"Why do you always do that?" I ask her.

"Do what?" she says.

"Insist I dive in."

"No one says you have to."

"Maybe you can explain to me what goading is."

Mom doesn't answer. It takes two to tango, and she doesn't want to fight.

When I think she's fallen asleep, I quietly slip into the water and duck under the dock. There, I tread water and watch her through the slats. When she realizes I'm gone, she sits up and calls out to me. When I don't respond, she calls out louder, sounding concerned.

"I'm right here," I say, and she peers down between her legs at me.

"What are you doing under there?"

"Looking up at you," I say.

"You're punishing me," she says, and she dives into the water.

We swim together across the lake and back. When we return to the dock the sun's too low in the sky to dry our suits so we change into our shorts and return to the dock to watch the sun fall behind the pine trees across the lake. It will be another two hours before it actually sets.

"My mother was always trying to make a lady out of me," Mom says, turning toward me as I sit beside her. "She felt my startling moves were unfeminine. I guess I make the same mistake, goading you into being rash."

"It's all right, Mom. It hasn't ruined me."

"I don't mean to be critical," Mom says, staring out across the lake.

"It's O.K.," I tell her, and Mom lets it go.

"Remember when there were no houses across there?" she says wistfully.

"I remember when the first one was built."

"The sound of that buzz saw all summer long."

"Well, there it goes," I say, as the sun disappears from our view.

While Mom collects pine cones from a clearing a stone's throw away, I take pictures of her. Sometimes when the light is just right, as it is now, her hair looks blonde, and I imagine my mother a young woman, not middle-aged.

We are sitting on the dock on two large inner tubes, eating our grilled hot dogs, when it grows dark and we can hardly see one another.

"Something unexpected has happened to me," Mom says with noticeable strain.

Here it comes, I think.

"I've met someone, Bern."

"A man?" I ask, hesitantly.

"No, a woman."

"Oh," I say relieved.

"Not *oh*," Mom says, mimicking my oh-that's-different tone.

"What do you mean?" I ask.

"I'm in love with her."

"You're in love with a woman?"

Mom waits a moment, then says, "Yes."

"I don't get it," I say, but of course I do.

"Her name is Gillian. She lives on Shelter Island. I asked you home to explain this to you."

God almighty, I think, no wonder Dad is angry. "Is this . . . something about you you've always known?"

"I'm not sure, Bern."

"How can you not be sure?"

"I know it seems incredible. It does to me, too . . . but I can't say I'm really surprised."

"It surprises me," I say. "How did it happen?"

"It just did, Bern. It just does."

"I mean, how did you meet?"

"We met on Shelter Island. I went out there to get away for a few days, and as luck would have it, it rained the whole time. There I was, stuck indoors, until finally I thought the hell with it and went for a long walk. I passed a farm stand and noticed it was open. Gillian has gardens and a greenhouse and sells flowers and vegetables. She told me I was the first person she'd seen in days, and before long I was drinking hot tea with her and telling her why I needed a respite."

"What's her story?" I ask.

Mom doesn't answer immediately. When she does, she says, "She's a lesbian."

"Did she tell you that?"

"Yes. I don't remember exactly how it came up, but I do remember being very interested."

"My god, Mom."

"I know this is a lot to digest."

"Dad knows, of course. That's why you and he aren't talking."

"A few days after I got home I got a call from her."

"She hasn't been to the house, has she?"

"No."

"Thank god!"

"I think I've said enough for now. We can talk more tomorrow."

Mom starts to get up and I say, "I thought I knew everything important there was to know about you."

"What made you think that?" she says.

"I'm afraid to ask what's to come of all this."

Mom carries her plate over to the pump and rinses it off. I don't expect an answer to my remark. If I want an answer from my mom I have to ask a question.

It's dark in the cabin, so we light a lamp and don't speak as we go through the motions of getting ready for bed. After undressing, I hang my clothes on a peg and put my pajamas on. Mom hunts down a book to read, then comes over to me and gives me a kiss goodnight on the cheek. She does this as naturally as she ever has, and I can't help but wonder how she can be so the same when she seems so different to me.

"Try not to think about this too much," she says. "Don't stay awake half the night asking yourself questions you can't answer.

They'll keep until tomorrow."

"I'll try not to," I say.

Mom takes the lamp up to the loft with her, and I lie down on the bunk. *Don't think about it?* She drops a bomb like that, then says don't think about it?

Mom is aware of my restlessness below her, and instead of snuffing out the light when she closes her book, she comes down to see me. I pull my legs up so she can sit on the foot of the bunk.

We say nothing to one another for the longest time, then in a low voice that saddens me, Mom says, "Ever since I met Gillian I've been in a struggle with my conscience, asking myself how I truly feel, and what I want, and what's the right thing to do. At times I thought I was losing my mind. I tried to put Gillian out of my mind and couldn't. I looked for things about her I don't like, but there is too much that I love. And I realized I wasn't struggling to decide anything. I'd already made a choice—I just hadn't acted on it because I was scared. Scared of the consequences, scared about everyone's future."

"What will you do?" I ask, staring at Mom's bare feet on the floor.

"I can't stay with your father when I'd rather be with someone else."

Images of Mom flash in my mind: Mom hanging laundry up in the basement on a rainy day, Mom making Jeff a birthday cake, Mom refinishing a chest that is to go in my room, Mom cutting Dad's hair.

"Where will you live?" I ask.

"For the time being at home. Your dad is going to England to work with John Beddoes."

"Is that a coincidence?"

"I think he asked John."

"I'm afraid of what's going to happen to him," I say.

"Each of us has to take care of ourselves, Bern. Life comes down to that sooner or later, and he will."

"I feel so sad."

"It's late. You won't feel quite so sad in the morning." Mom pats my leg as she gets up from the couch. "Try to sleep now. Try to do that as hard as you try to do so many other things."

Of course trying to sleep is the last thing in the world one should do if they want to fall asleep. I lay awake stewing for another hour before sleep overcomes me.

The next morning Mom is up and dressed before me. I stand at the cabin door and look out at her on the dock and try to imagine a woman sitting beside her. It's easier to imagine Meg than Chris. Meg Benson has a daughter who is schizophrenic, and she and Mom have spent long hours discussing their individual tragedies. But they have spent more hours discussing books they have read and the summer garden they share. The Bensons live next door. Between their house and ours is a disputed piece of land which was turned into a common garden.

Chris and Ted Rooney know Mom and Dad through the yacht club. I've never understood the friendship between Chris and Mom. With all the privileges of her class, Chris has curiously never been at a loss for someone to envy. I've always suspected she had a thing for my dad, and instead of being irked by that, Mom felt sorry for Chris. Chris is a writer, and a good one. I suppose that makes up for a lot, but my instinct and common sense tell me Gillian is more like Meg.

When I open the door, Mom hears the squeak and looks up. "Whatcha doing?" I call out to her.

"Waiting for you," she says. "Get dressed, and let's take the boat out."

After changing into shorts I grab a couple of bananas and my camera.

"Bring me my sunglasses!" Mom hollers to me, and I reach for a pair of badly scratched sunglasses off the card table.

"How long have you had these?" I ask, handing Mom's glasses over to her and stepping into the boat.

"Ten, twelve years," she answers.

"I thought so."

"They're the same style as yours, Miss Fashion Plate."

"I wasn't commenting on their style," I say, and we push off from the dock.

I row the boat to a favorite spot where birch trees overhang the water, then let the boat coast and eat a banana. When Jeff and I were kids we would get up in the trunk split of the tallest birch and jump from there into the water, aiming for the center of our inner tube. The only real danger was getting scraped by the valve as we hit our target. Not far from this spot, twenty yards offshore, large rocks, resting on the bottom, reach nearly to the surface of the water. Jeff and I would swim out to them and try to walk on their slippery surface, hoping someone would see us and think we were walking on the water. Jeff knew that spot well, which made it hard to understand how he could have forgotten about it the day of his accident.

It was July fourth weekend, Jeff's birthday weekend, and Dad had bought Jeff a motor boat. Dad wanted to get Jeff a sailboat for his thirteen birthday, but Jeff wanted a boat he could water ski from.

It was on its maiden voyage that Jeff crashed the boat onto the rocks. Dad was with him and was able to rescue Jeff from the water, but Jeff had hit his head on the boat, or the rocks, and Dad couldn't resuscitate him until he got him ashore. A couple, who were vacationing on the lake, helped Dad give Jeff CPR until the paramedics arrived. Mom and I had no idea that any of this was going on. After more than an hour and no sight of them, we went out in the rowboat to haul them in for lunch and found the motorboat, but not Dad or Jeff. The couple who had helped Dad heard our screams and told us Dad and Jeff were at the local hospital. I never knew what happened to Jeff's boat, if it sank to the bottom of the lake or someone had salvaged it.

"Is this because of Jeff?" I say to Mom.

"Did I fall in love with Gillian because of Jeff?" Mom asks me.

"He could have something to do with it," I say.

"My loving Gillian isn't about Jeff or your Dad. It's about me."

I remind Mom that after Jeff's accident she moved to the guest room, and she says, "Your father and I were changed by the accident."

"I didn't think it was so you wouldn't wake Dad in the middle of the night." Mom doesn't confirm or deny this. "Who will have custody of Jeff?" I ask.

"Your father will."

"Why him? He can't take care of Jeff, not full-time."

"Because he's the one who can't let go."

Our rowboat has coasted away from the shoreline, and I have to squint to see Mom. "What does that mean?" I ask, "that you can?"

"I've wanted to," Mom says.

"I didn't know that," I say surprised. "How come you never told me?"

"Because your father is alone enough, he doesn't need us siding against him."

I take a hold of the oars and start to row. After several strokes I ask, "Why does Dad hold on?"

"He's hoping for a miracle, or some medical advance," Mom says, her voice emotional. I wish the sun were not shining in my eyes and I could see her expression.

"After all these years?" I say, and then, because my stomach is growling, I head the boat toward shore.

Mom suggests we go for a swim when we reach the dock. Instead of getting my bathing suit, I take off my clothes and jump in naked. Mom does the same. I try to float on my back the way Mom can, but first my feet, then my legs sink, and I go under. I don't know how she does it unless she's part otter.

That afternoon, Mom and I roll out two rickety bikes I thought she'd junked years ago and bicycle into town. The tires on mine are nearly flat, so we stop at a gas station to fill them. Mom loses two quarters in the Coke machine and asks the attendant if he will reimburse her.

He says, "Air ain't free," and Mom answers, "Since when?"

"Since I bought this place," the man says, winking, maybe hoping Mom will think he's cute. Boy has he got a wrong number.

After browsing around town, we enter Woody's, a bar and grill with sawdust on the floor and flashing beer signs over the bar. Dad always hated to come here. He said it was because of the greasy food, but more than likely it was the atmosphere which offended him. Dad's scene was the yacht club.

Mom and I order cheeseburgers with the works. While we're waiting for them I tell her about a photo essay I did for the *Village Voice*. She gazes off, not listening to me, and I shut up.

There was a time when Jeff was first home from the hospital when Mom would stare like this, and nothing I or anyone said could bring her around. I was very angry with Mom then for abandoning me. One day, when I found her sitting with Jeff, I told her Jeff wasn't there, that he'd been upstairs with me all afternoon. I expected Mom to be hurt. I wanted to hurt her. But she turned to me and said, "I hope so."

"What does she look like?" I ask.

"She's dark," Mom says.

"Tall? Short? Fat? Skinny?"

"She's attractive," Mom answers, her infatuation apparent.

"That attractive?" I say. "What do you two do together?"

"Oh, I don't know, Bern."

"Come on."

"No, you're mad at me. I can hear it in your voice."

"I'm jealous," I say.

"Is that it?" Mom asks.

"You weren't listening to me. You were staring off into space, thinking about her."

"I'm sorry, Bern. Let's try again."

Instead of telling her about the photo essay, I talk briefly about my trip to California, avoiding the part that would give me away. I'm two weeks late getting my period and I'm afraid I might be pregnant. Sharing that with Mom, at this time, somehow seems inappropriate. Or maybe I don't want to admit that I've been foolishly romantic.

Our cheeseburgers arrive, and we eat like wolves. Mom says we have time to make the show in town if I'm interested, and we pass up the homemade cherry pie to save room for popcorn at the movies. As the lights fade in the theater Mom asks me if I would like to go out to Shelter Island with her to meet Gillian.

"God, no!" I say.

"Why not?" Mom asks.

The woman seated behind us shushes us loudly, and Mom whispers, "Why not?"

"I haven't the nerve," I whisper back. We are shushed again, so Mom lets it go until we are back at the cabin.

We are floating in our inner tubes off the dock when Mom asks, "Why haven't you the nerve?" I tell her I just don't, and she reminds me of the summer I learned to dive off the dock. I remember I did that for her. I have done all the scary things in my life for her.

"I'd like to meet Gillian," I say, "but not on Shelter Island. Maybe some place neutral."

"I understand," Mom says.

Under the cover of darkness I ask Mom if she considers herself a lesbian.

"I'm in love with a woman," she says.

"Were you ever in love with Dad?"

"When I had you and Jeff I was."

"You aren't just saying that so I won't feel lousy?"

She gets out of the water, tosses me the soap, and says, "I was once in love with Bill."

Sometime later Mom returns to the dock in her pajamas. "Enough of that, Bern."

"Enough of what?" I ask.

"Trying to figure out your mom."

"You don't know that's what I'm doing," I say.

"What are you doing?" she asks.

I don't tell Mom I've been crying in the dark because I feel I've lost the only member of my family I'm close to, the one I thought I knew.

Early the next morning, before either of us is up and dressed, someone bangs on the cabin door and hollers in to us that Mom is to call home immediately.

We dress quickly and take the Citroen to town. My first thought is that Jeff is in some crisis.

In the general store I stand beside Mom at the telephone.

"Why today," she says into the receiver. "What did she say?... Why didn't you speak to her?... But I thought you said you called her.... O.K., Bill.... All right, we'll be home in a couple hours."

There goes my day with Mom, I think. "What is it?" I ask as soon as she hangs up the phone.

She thanks the store owner on our way out. Once outside, she tells me Dad has to leave immediately for England and can't get a nurse for Jeff.

Packing up the car I think, the more things change the more they stay the same.

Once we're on the road Mom says she's sorry I'm not going to get a real visit with Dad.

"I'm not," I say.

"Why's that?" Mom asks me.

"It isn't like you to play dumb, Mom."

"You're mad at me, aren't you?"

"I'm mad at you both. Nice visit," I say sarcastically. "My first night home the two of you disappear without even saying goodnight to me and I'm left downstairs wondering what the hell's going on and if I did something to offend you or if you just don't give a damn about me."

"I'm sorry, Bern."

"Yeah, sure. Well I'm going back to the city tomorrow."

Mom turns off the main road and takes the back roads to Bridgeport, stopping at every fruit stand she sees.

The summer after Jeff's accident Mom and I went up to the cabin for two weeks. I don't recall anything unusual we did that would make those weeks seem other than ordinary to anyone else, but to us they were extraordinary, and we were sad when they were over. We knew the magic, whatever it was, would not follow us home. Along the way we stopped at every produce stand, and I remember thinking how hurt Dad would be if he could see how reluctant we were to return home.

When Mom and I arrive at the house we find Dad is gone and

a nurse is with Jeff. Mom's understanding was that Dad couldn't get a nurse, that he would be waiting for us to spell him.

The nurse hands Mom a note from Dad. After reading it, Mom gives it to me. Dad says he left on the early flight because there were no seats on the later one. He doesn't say good-bye, or that he's sorry for leaving without saying good-bye, or when we will hear from him.

"I thought you weren't available," Mom says to the nurse.

"I'm not," she answers. "I'm late to another patient."

As Mom sees the nurse out, I go upstairs with my bags. When I return downstairs Mom tells me Gillian will arrive in two hours.

"Why'd you do that?" I ask her.

"Because you're leaving tomorrow."

"Is it necessary I meet her?"

"You said you would like to."

"I was being polite, and I only threatened to leave tomorrow because I was mad that our time alone had been interrupted."

"I'm sorry, Bern. I misunderstood. We will have some time alone if you stay."

"Mom, I'm not ready for this."

"What is *this?*" she asks.

"This is Gillian, the woman my mother is in love with, the woman she is leaving my father for. Isn't that enough?"

"I thought you were ready."

"You expect way too much of me, Mom. You treat me like I were you. You did that when I was a kid and you still do. I'm not you. When are you going to realize that?"

Mom sinks down on the couch in the library, and I turn away from her to walk over to the porch door. After a long silence she says, "You're right, Bern, I have pushed you. I pushed you to dive off the dock, to ride a bike before you wanted to, to take the hardest courses in school, and now to meet Gillian. And I did it for me, not for you...because I wasn't encouraged to do or be anything. If you proved to be as good as anyone then I might believe I was."

"I'm sorry," I say, and I walk over to her and sit down on the couch beside her. "You know, I'm proud of the things I can do because of you. It's just that at times, I still want you to protect me... and excuse me."

Mom puts her arm around me and hugs me to her.

An hour later, as I'm setting the table in the library, I hear Mom knocking about in the kitchen and I go to see what she's up to. She's mopping up the kitchen floor in a pair of dress pants and a silk blouse.

"What are you doing?" I ask.

"What's it look like I'm doing?"

"Why don't you let me since you're all dolled up?" Mom shoos me away. She's nervous. She cleans when she's nervous.

As I settle onto the couch in the library, the doorbell rings. I listen for the other voice in the hall, but all I can hear is Mom. The two women enter the library smiling. Mom's hand lightly touches Gillian's arm as she introduces Gillian to me. I'm not expecting someone as beautiful and sexually appealing as Gillian, and I worry that my astonishment shows.

Gillian comments on how much Mom and I look alike, and Mom steps away from Gillian to put her arm around me. "Just as outspoken, too," she says. I haven't said a word, so Mom's remark is rather ironic.

I finally manage a "Nice to meet you." Mom sees I'm nervous and gives my hand a gentle squeeze, then leads us onto the porch. Gillian and I each take a chair, avoiding the porch swing, and Mom leaves us to bring out a tray of cold drinks. As the scent of expensive perfume wafts in my direction, my mind races for something to say. Gillian's the kind of woman who wears expensive lingerie, too, I think. And a nightgown to bed, not pajamas.

"I'm sorry you and Jean had to leave the cabin early," she says.

"Would you like to see Mom and Meg's garden?" I ask.

Mom joins us, and the three of us step off the porch and walk across the lawn. Mom puts her arm around Gillian's waist. On their way back from the garden they walk separately, Mom carrying tomatoes, and Gillian with her hands in the pockets of her slacks, smiling at whatever Mom is saying to her.

I can't believe Mom does it to me again. She leaves Gillian and me to go serve dinner. I offer to help Mom and she says no. I ask Gillian if she would like to see the house and she says, "No, not just yet. This is pleasant, sitting here."

Pleasant for you, I think.

"Jean tells me you're a photographer."

"Yes."

"A photojournalist, I think she said."

I nod my head.

"For a newspaper?"

"Newspapers and magazines," I say. "And stock houses." I explain what a stock house is, then change the subject to get her attention off me. "Mom says you have a greenhouse."

"And a chicken coop," Gillian says.

"She didn't tell me about that."

"And a tennis court?"

"Not that either," I say.

"It's an asphalt-and-grass court, Gillian says, smiling. She has a warm smile. "Grass is growing where the asphalt's cracked."

It's hard to imagine Gillian having a chicken coop and a tennis court that's gone to seed. It isn't hard to imagine Mom loving such a place.

"Do you play tennis?" I ask.

"Not at home," she says, laughing softly.

"Are you any good?"

"Your mother asked me the same question. I told her she'd have to play me to find out, and so will you."

"Anyone hungry?" Mom asks.

I leap up, relieved to have something to do.

At the table Gillian asks me what Mom and I did up at the cabin. Surely she knows why Mom took me up there.

"The usual stuff," I say.

Gillian doesn't pursue me. Instead, she tells Mom about the cutting garden she's putting in for a friend, and without realizing it when it happens, I'm relaxed and having a good time listening to Mom and Gillian. Not until Mom announces that she is going to check on Jeff do I realize that for the better part of an hour I haven't thought of either Jeff or Dad, and that it has been pleasant not to think of them. As Mom steps away from the table she touches the back of Gillian's head with her hand. It's not something I ever saw Mom do to Dad. Gillian's eyes follow Mom out of the library, and I can feel the intensity of her gaze.

"I realize this isn't easy for you," Gillian says to me. I try to look like I haven't the foggiest notion what she's talking about, at the same time wondering why the hell she's pointed it up. "That's all," Gillian says. "I just thought I would say that."

"You haven't ever been married, have you?" I ask.

"No," she answers. "I was never interested in men romantically. I think I'm going to join your mother. Maybe I can help her. You want to come along?"

"No," I answer. Gillian has not yet seen Jeff, and I'm surprised that she shows no reluctance to do so, and that she doesn't feel she should wait until she's been invited. "You can take coffee in with you, if you'd like," I say. "Mom would probably like some. I'm sure it's brewing in the kitchen."

When Gillian leaves the library I get up from the table and go out for a walk. It's not yet dark out. I sit on the sea wall and decide I will get an abortion when I return to the city. I wouldn't want to marry Mark even if he were willing. I don't want to be a single parent, and with or without Mark, that is what I would be.

First thing in the morning Mom comes to my room. "I'm going down to fix breakfast. Are you joining us?"

"Us?" I say, surprised.

Mom's expression asks, Is something wrong with that? and I say, "I just didn't think she would be here."

Mom makes a move to leave the room, but I stop her.

"I am going to head back to the City today. I have hours of darkroom work to do."

"If Gillian weren't here would you want to stay?" Mom asks at the door.

"It's not her. I need some time alone to sort things out. And not just things here, but things in my own life."

"I'm sorry, Bern, we haven't talked enough about you."

"It's all right, Mom. I understand."

"It's not all right," she says. "It never has been."

"It's made me self-sufficient," I say, but without much conviction.

Mom answers, "Come down and have breakfast with me."

When I step into the kitchen the first face I see is Gillian's. I'm not yet seated when she excuses herself to go shower and dress, and I ask Mom if she told Gillian I was leaving. She nods her head, then asks me if I'm having a problem with something or someone other than she or Gillian.

"I'm wrestling with something," I say, "but I've decided to wrestle with it alone."

"Are you sure?"

"Yes, I can take care of this."

On my way upstairs to get my things I pass Gillian on her way down. I'm too confused emotionally to speak.

three

I'm back in the
City two days when I
get my period. Instead of feeling
relieved, I feel sad and lonely. The thought
that a baby might be growing inside me was
not all bad. I'm not a young woman without property
position or loving companionship, but I do understand that girl's
desire for a child.

And I'm not unlike my dad, I think, as I measure and pour developer and fixer, instead of a drink, then put a tape on and spend the night in my darkroom, printing and toning the Sonoma pictures to Chopin.

Many photographers don't do their own printing. I do. When I'm in the darkroom I escape from time and vanish into the work. The printing quiets my mind, inspires me when it is effortless, and challenges me because I will never be able to master it.

On one of the Sonoma rolls there are several pictures of Mark. Days later I will send them to him, without keeping even one for myself.

Wistfulness was the emotion which flowed in my home during my adolescent years. I wanted a bright joy. I thought I found that when I found Mark, but I had not. Always, following the excitement of being with Mark, was disappointment that Mark and

I were only playmates. It would take more time and integrity before I would realize that I was as poor a match for Mark as he was for me, that my attraction to him increased with his resistance and therefore had more to do with my ego than my heart.

In the City I try to put Mom and Gillian out of my mind, but Mom writes letters about the two of them. My first reaction is to wonder why she is doing this to me. Why she doesn't leave me alone. Then, why I say I want to be left alone and behave otherwise. I reread some passages a dozen times.

From Old Field

Dear Bern,

It's Tuesday, noon. Gillian left only hours ago for Shelter Island. She was here three days, enough time for me to be spoiled by her constant company. I've been cleaning the house since to keep from feeling lonesome, and just now sat down with a ham sandwich. . . .

Dear Bern,

We had a scene here this weekend. Chris came over to give me her latest book. To make a long story short, she insulted Gillian, asking her what kind of woman she was?! I usually let Chris go on with her nonsense until she runs out of steam but this time I told her to shut up, and she ran from the house, wounded. Gillian was stung by the remark, but not badly hurt. Neither she nor I were surprised. What kind of world is this when rudeness and cruelty no longer surprise us?

From Shelter Island

Dear Bern,

Gillian is downstairs cooking our dinner while I rest

in her childhood room. On my first visit here, Gillian told me that as a youngster she would stand on the bed when she was supposed to be taking a nap and look out the window at her grandmother's geese. At the time we were standing at the window, looking down at Gillian's flower garden in bloom. She put her hand on my back, and when I turned to her she kissed me. At forty-seven years old one can still be pleasantly surprised.

Dear Bern,

Gillian has gone next door to help Mrs. Yeager put a crib up for a grandchild who will be visiting over Thanksgiving. I was invited along, but it's so nice not having to see anyone that I begged off.

I got a letter from your dad yesterday telling me he was no longer living with the Beddoes, that he'd taken a flat so he could entertain privately. He might have hoped to get my goat, but I feel relieved more than anything else that he might be seeing someone.

From Old Field

Dear Bern,

Gillian is asleep beside me. She exhausted herself driving up to Cazenovia and back today to see a friend in crisis. I wouldn't have imagined that old Chevy of hers could make such a trip. The woman Gillian went to see was once her lover. They have remained close friends. Gillian's and my pasts couldn't be more different, and sometimes it takes as much imagination as willingness to understand one another. Gillian had her first relationship with a woman when she was eighteen years old, and more than I care to know about since then. She can't get

over that I've been married all these years and have a grown daugh-
ter. I'm not sure if this means she's enchanted or horrified. I don't think
she envies my past as I sometimes do hers.

Dear Bern,

We had a heavy snow last week. Unusual for November. For two
days Gillian and I stayed cozy inside, cooked delicious meals, sat around
and listened to music, read, and played dominoes. Then, today, we got
out the snowshoes and went over to Harbor Hills. I'm sure you can im-
agine its quiet beauty. For a moment I felt nostalgic for the past when
you and Jeff were youngsters and your dad and I would take you over
there tobogganing.

Why don't you come home for Christmas?. . .

Mom is waiting for me Christmas Eve at the Port Jefferson station. It is cold, but there is no snow. November's snow melted weeks
ago. Mom hurries me to the car and coasts through a couple of stop
signs on the drive home.

"Did you leave something on the stove?" I ask. Mom is puzzled
by the question. She's not aware that her tempo is several beats faster
than most people's.

I see the house from a distance. The front bushes are trimmed
with lights. Candles are lit in every window. An enormous wreath
is on the front door, and I will soon discover that others, nearly as
extravagant, are at the side and back doors.

"Gillian must have had some time on her hands," I say to Mom
as we step into the hall.

Inside, the house is decorated as I have never seen it. Pine boughs climb the banister. More boughs are on the mantels, and a tree in the library is decorated with familiar ribbons and ornaments. Gillian is nowhere in sight.

"She is here, isn't she?" I ask.

"She's in with Jeff," Mom explains. "I'll tell her we're home."

Gillian hears Mom and me in the library and comes into the room and over to me with her arms out, offering me a hug. She is warm and strong, and I enjoy the affectionate greeting. "We've been looking forward to you," she says.

"You've been busy little beavers," I say.

"The gardening business is slow in the winter."

I head in the direction Gillian came from. It isn't like me to go see Jeff without any prompting, and Mom looks surprised. "I'm curious to see what she's done to him," I say, but Mom knows better. I'm running away to collect myself.

Jeff looks the same. Awake, his eyes are wandering about the room. When they land on me they show no recognition. I step over to Jeff and lay my hand on his forehead. The old sadness awakens in me. I cannot imagine what it is like for my mother to live with this sadness every day of her life, but I have deep respect for her and I am glad now that she has Gillian's help.

Mom comes into the room with an eggnog for me and suggests we keep Gillian company in the kitchen.

"She's fixing dinner too?" I ask.

"It's an overture."

"She doesn't need to do that," I say.

Mom puts her arm around me and kisses my cheek. "Thanks for coming home," she says.

Over a roast beef dinner, Mom tells Gillian I'm having a show at Marcuse Pfeifer in the fall, and Gillian asks if she can see some of my photos.

"Of course," I answer. "I'm surprised she hasn't showed you some. Not even *Missing Parts?*" I ask, looking to Mom.

"That's for you to do," she says.

"And you thought her wardrobe was the only thing old-fashioned about her," I say to Gillian, and Mom laughs. God it feels good, good to laugh with Mom. I'm much too serious when I'm not around her.

After dinner Mom hunts up *Missing Parts*. One of the photos in the series is of her. Not long after Mom had her right breast removed, she and Meg were out back, putting in the vegetable garden. It was something Mom had dreamed and planned and talked about during those weeks she was in the hospital, then recovering at home. I could tell, watching her that day, that she was hurting, but she kept at it cheerfully. I could also tell, watching Dad that day, that Mom's indomitable spirit in the face of such difficulty annoyed him.

That afternoon, when Mom went into the house to shower, I followed her. She came out of the bathroom with a towel wrapped around her, still damp from her shower, and smiled at me, a little surprised to see me lying on her bed.

"May I see it?" I said.

"My breast?" she asked, and I nodded my head.

Mom removed her towel and stepped over to me. The scar was still red and sore-looking. "Does it hurt?" I asked.

"Not much."

"Can I take a picture of you like that?"

Mom said yes without hesitation. She stood with her back to the open door as I focused Jeff's camera on her.

Before I could take a second picture, Dad stepped into the room. "What are you doing to her?" he said, shocked. Mom's back was to him, and she flinched. I wanted to run from the room, but Dad grabbed hold of my arm.

"Let her go," Mom said. "I asked her to take my picture."

"Why would you do that?" Dad said.

"It's very personal," Mom answered.

"It's very peculiar," Dad said, letting go of my arm.

The other photos in the series are a man with one leg playing a fiddle while his wife dances for him; a woman with no teeth singing in a church choir; a boy with one arm posing with his bowling ball for the camera; and a young girl who is blind, sewing the hem of a dress.

"Mom was my inspiration," I say when Gillian compliments my work.

"I'm sure she's as proud of you," Gillian says, and we both glance at Mom, who looks quite serious.

"I just aim and shoot," I say.

"Would you take some pictures of us?" Gillian asks.

I don't hesitate to jump up and get my camera.

"I don't think she meant right now," Mom says.

"Yes," I answer. "Now's good. But go put your pajamas on."

I was wrong about Gillian, she did wear pajamas.

I have a field day over the next two days, taking pictures of Mom and Gillian at the breakfast table, Mom with Jeff, Gillian with Jeff, Mom wrapping a gift, Gillian asleep on the couch, Mom putting the turkey in the oven, Mom shouting at me to get away with that camera, I'm in her way, and Gillian blowing me a kiss as I depart.

Jeff's first Christmas after the accident, Dad carried him out to the couch in the library so he would be with us when we opened our gifts. I had no present for Jeff, and I was ashamed and confused by his joining us. When Dad asked me to set up the camera and join him and Mom around the couch, I refused. I said I didn't know how to work the self-timer. Dad tried to figure it out but couldn't.

Mom probably knew how but didn't try. I took a picture of Mom and Dad with Jeff.

The following year, when Dad carried Jeff out to the couch, I disappeared. Mom found me in the trunk room. I told her Dad's pretending Jeff was O.K. made me feel funny, and she promised me there'd be no pictures that year.

I wonder, as I photograph Gillian on the couch opening her present from Mom, if Mom is remembering past Christmases.

My last morning at home I go into the dining room to say good-bye to Mom. Gillian is there. She tells me Mom wants me to wake her.

"She's still in bed?" I ask surprised. Mom never slept in. She had to get up to take care of Jeff.

Gillian answers yes.

"Dad never did this," I say. "Not first thing in the morning."

"I'm happy to help," Gillian says, matter of factly.

"No one should have to," I say, feeling irritable suddenly. "And Jeff shouldn't be stuck this way. But Dad won't let anyone off the hook. Now you're on it, too."

"It's not difficult for me," Gillian says. "It's nothing compared to what your mother does for me."

"What's that?" I ask, and Gillian says, "If I tell you, you'll be embarrassed."

"Oh, god, then don't."

Gillian laughs brightly, then says, "Your mother is a beautiful woman and has immense energy. I love watching her do just about anything."

"Beautiful?" I say. "I've always thought of Mom as handsome, not beautiful. You're what I'd call beautiful," I say, surprising myself as well as Gillian.

"It takes all kinds," she says, recovering better than I do.

As I start to leave Gillian says, "Will you come out to Shelter Island some weekend?"

I nod my head, but Gillian looks unsure. "Yes," I say. "I'd like to."

Mom is making the bed when I step into her room.

"I'm taking off now. You don't have to drive me to the station, I'll call a cab."

"I'm all set, Bern."

"You're not even dressed."

"It'll take you longer to collect your things," she answers, and she's right.

At the station, Mom hugs me good-bye.

"Thanks again," I say. "It was wonderful. She's wonderful."

"I'm lucky to have you both," Mom answers.

"Yeah, you probably are," I say.

Mom's letters continue after Christmas.

From Old Field

Dear Bern,

The Kobell boy came by this morning to ask if he could shovel the driveway for me. I sprained my wrist a couple of days ago, lifting Jeff, and have let the snow pile up. Afterward, I invited him in for some hot chocolate and asked him how come he wasn't in school. He said he hadn't gone because he needed to make some money. I gave him another ten dollars and told him if he didn't get an education he'd need a lot of good will. He smiled, not understanding what the hell I meant. When he left I broke down. It was the peach fuzz growing on his cheeks which saddened me. It reminded me of Jeff's adolescence—watching all the changes take place as though everything were normal. I know that was a hard time for you as well, and my self-absorbing pain didn't help matters. I'm sorry, Bern.

Dear Bern,

Meg called this morning to ask me to dinner. I accepted her offer and took the opportunity to tell her and Bob about Gillian. Bob was uncomfortable hearing I love another woman, but Meg was not. I feel good that Meg knows. I don't like pretending to be something I'm not.

Dear Bern,

Ted Rooney is in the hospital with a gastric ulcer and has been told he must stop drinking.

I didn't know how it would be seeing Chris after the blowup we had, but nothing was said about that, and Chris seemed glad to have my company.

We've had more than a week of cold rain, and everything is an ugly gray color. A spring rain at least promises wildflowers and green lawns. This drizzle promises absolutely nothing. Maybe I've spent too many hours with Chris. I'm beginning to sound like her. Forgive me.

Dear Bern,

Last weekend seems a long time ago. Friday night when I arrived at Gillian's, she said she'd been doing some serious thinking and had decided she didn't want to be responsible for the breakup of my marriage. I said it was ridiculous for her to think that she was breaking up my marriage, that she was not the cause, and she got upset with me for saying she was being ridiculous. I left the farmhouse before we had dinner, telling myself all the way home that leaving was the only sensible thing to do.

The next day I kept busy packing clothes to send to your father, bringing firewood in from the garage, and cleaning out the kitchen cabinets and drawers. I found a pencil with Dink's Hardware stamped on it in the junk drawer and remembered the day I got that with my three gallons of Chinese red paint to cover the walls in the library. I was young, just married, and full of big ideas and ambitious plans of how I was going to redo the house. I was happy then. That the same things don't make me happy now doesn't mean those were false times, or that I'm now false. But how do I explain this to Gillian? And what if her problem with me is something more difficult to resolve?

I miss her terribly, I'm sorry I left, and I wish she would answer her phone. . . .

Dear Bern,

Each February it is hard for me to believe that March will ever come, and with it spring. But it always does. Saturday, Gillian and I packed a picnic basket and drove up to the cabin for the day and night. It's beautiful up there now. There aren't any flowers yet, but the air is rich with the smell of pine, and the lake is calm.

We spread a blanket out on the dock and ate a picnic lunch. The water was ice cold so Gillian wouldn't go in for a swim with me. Later we had a long talk. I built a fire, and we cuddled up in front of it. I'm sure I will get used to Gillian one day, but at the moment that is hard to imagine. Gillian told me she was less concerned about breaking up my marriage than she was concerned *it could not be broken, that what Bill and I have gone through has cemented us. I told her I have been alone for ten years. . .*

From Shelter Island

Dear Bern,

I'm just out of a hot bath where I soaked for over an hour after a hard day of work. This morning Gillian and I replaced roof shingles blown off in the last rainstorm, then got out her small tractor and plowed the gardens. It felt awfully good to bend and stretch and lift as we did. Physical exertion has always been my remedy for whatever ails me.

Do you remember me asking you to clean out the trunk room the day your hamster died? I thought the physical activity would help you cope with your heartache, but instead you made a nest for yourself in there to hide from your cruel mom. If nothing else I have shown you how imperfect love can be, certainly how imperfect I am.

From Old Field

Dear Bern,

Just up from the basement. All it seems I've done lately is muck it out. I don't remember a wetter spring.

Chris and Ted are having problems. Chris called me after I'd gone to bed last night. I feel sorry for Chris because she doesn't have a closer friend. When I got to Chris' it was after two in the morning. Ted was gone, and Chris had a red welt on her cheek. I asked her if Ted had hit her. She couldn't bring herself to say he had, but she didn't say he hadn't. I said I was sorry. If Chris stopped drinking she would probably not feel she had to

*put up with Ted's drinking behavior, and yet look at me.
Unfortunately, people can tolerate a great deal of un-
pleasantness and abuse.*

Dear Bern,

 *The time has come for me to correct my life. I've
written to your father to tell him I've filed for a divorce
and will be moving into the farmhouse whether or not
he returns. I would rather have done this once he was
home, but although he mentions in each of his letters that
he plans to return, he never says when. It's possible he
would wait forever for me to ask him to come back. I
wouldn't wait forever for anyone.*

 *I'll find a long-term care facility for Jeff if your fa-
ther doesn't return and agree to take care of him.*

 *I don't know how you feel about this, but I do know
this is not the first time you have been disappointed in
your parents. . . .*

Days later I get a call from Gillian. I am on my way out to take
some photos and stop to pick up the phone. I don't remember her
words. I'm not sure she spoke clearly, or at all. Maybe she was crying. I knew at once, by some hideous insight, that something terrible had happened to Mom.

The night before, on her way to Shelter Island, Mom was in
a head-on collision and killed.

After hanging up the phone with Gillian, nothing I see or touch
or hear for many hours will seem to have any relevance to me. It
is as though I am severed from life. When I arrive at Port Jefferson
station I don't recognize Gillian. She doesn't wait for me to act. She
hurries over and puts her arms around me. Holding me close, she

says she's sorry over and over again. I don't remember telling Gillian what train I would be taking. I don't remember telling her anything.

We walk to the car and are quiet on the drive home. I gaze out the window at the blur of landscape, and, because I cannot yet accept reality, I think it is Mom who is driving me home from the station. It is natural to think this. It has occurred so many times it takes no thinking at all. When I turn to say something to Mom and see it is Gillian beside me, terror rises up in me. I will remember the damp smell of Gillian's Chevy whenever I miss Mom.

"We're home," Gillian says. "You've got your father's flight information. And you have a car, don't you? You don't need mine?"

"Don't leave me," I say.

Gillian looks startled but says, "All right, I can stay for a little while."

"Where is she?" I ask.

"At the funeral home."

"Will you take me there?"

Gillian looks at me sadly.

"I don't want to go alone," I say.

Gillian drives me to the funeral home, waits outside for me, and an hour later, when we return to the house, she walks me to the front door. Her eyes are dry, but the look of gravity in them is hard to bear.

"I'll be at the farmhouse if you need me," she says.

"Oh, god," I cry, and Gillian and I hug one another. "I thought no more bad things could happen."

"Bern, you can call me anytime and come out. I don't think I should come here. I've written down directions in case you need to get away." Gillian hands me a folded piece of paper. As she starts to turn away I ask her when she saw Mom last. She doesn't say at the hospital. Instead, she tells me, "Last weekend, and she was very happy, especially about you. Your acceptance of her put her at ease about herself and you."

"How are we going—" I start to say and can't finish. Gillian takes my hand and squeezes it. Because she doesn't take me into her arms I know I must let her go, and I do.

Once inside, I hurry upstairs, then stand for an anxious moment in the middle of my room at a loss. I don't know what to do. I head for my bathroom, go through it to the guest room, and close the door to the hallway. The closet in the guest room is empty and so are the dresser drawers. I lift the bedspread and see that the bed has been stripped. Where are Mom's things, I wonder, and I tear out of the room and down the hall. Her clothes are in the hamper in the room my parents once shared. I take a shirt of hers and hurry back to my room. Jeff's nurse surprises me in the hallway, and I hide Mom's shirt behind my back.

"I heard you come in," the nurse says. "Do you want me to stay? Miss Eames said you might."

"Yes, please stay."

"She said your father would be home this evening. Do you think he will want me to stay the night?"

"Yes—no, he'll probably take care of Jeff. But stay until he comes, just in case?"

"I'll plan to stay the night," the nurse says, and when she turns, I go into my room and lie down on the bed. My body is shaking. I curl up in a ball, hugging Mom's shirt to me.

At the airport hours later, I imagine people are staring at me. I'm sure I look strange because I feel so strange. Every seat in Customs is taken. I stand at the glass partition.

There he is, I say to myself when I see Dad. He has on a dark overcoat, and his shoulders are rounded. He squints, trying to find me in the crowd. I wave.

Dad's face is gray, his voice emotionless. "Who's with Jeff?" he asks me.

"A nurse," I say.

We don't talk again until we are on the expressway. Dad asks, "Where's Jean?"

"She's at the funeral home."

"What's being done?"

"What you said, Dad." Until that moment I had forgotten that I had called Morris Funeral Home and given them his instructions.

"Have you called anyone?" Dad asks.

"No, you can do that, can't you?"

We don't go directly home. Dad asks me to take him to the funeral home. I can tell he's disappointed when I say I'll wait for him in the car, but it doesn't make me less determined to do so.

I wish now I hadn't asked Gillian to take me to see Mom. It wasn't her. To begin with, her hair was combed strangely to cover her head wound. And her face was powdered and rouged. Mom never wore makeup—she had a natural ruddiness. But worst of all, her hands lay folded across her chest in a passive and saintly gesture. Mom was passionate and imperfect, and I wanted to remember her that way. Alone in the car, I start to cry and cry hard, then, frightened I won't be able to stop if I let myself go on, I get out of the car and walk down the block.

Three teenaged boys are sitting on the hood of a car in front of the ice-cream shop, teasing some girls who are seated at one of the sidewalk tables. The girls are enjoying the attention. I walk past them to Hackett's drugstore, wishing I could jump out of my skin and into any one of theirs. They seem so invincible and are having such a good time.

Mr. Hackett is mopping up the floor of his store. I duck out of sight so he won't see me. At the end of the block I cross the street and walk down to a red brick office building with tall steps.

I once took dance lessons in this building and afterward would sit on the steps and wait for Mom to pick me up. Sometimes she would be late and it would get dark, but I wouldn't dare cross the street and wait for her in front of the well-lit funeral home. I hated her when she poked fun of me for being a scaredy cat. No, that's not true. I didn't hate Mom. I loved her more than I loved anyone.

I see Dad come out of the funeral home and head for the car. I don't get up from the steps immediately. When I cross the street and join him he doesn't ask me where I was and I don't say.

At home, Dad and I go see Jeff. Dad puts a tape on, then steps over to Jeff to kiss him. "Have you told him?" Dad asks me.

I shake my head no.

Dad pulls a chair up close to the bed. He sits down on it and takes a hold of Jeff's hand, then kisses it and looks into Jeff's vacant eyes. "I have some bad news, kiddo. Mom was in an automobile accident. A drunk driver hit her head-on, then ran from the scene. She didn't make it, Jeffrey."

Had I told this to Dad, or was he making up a story for Jeff? I reach out and touch the bedcover over Jeff's legs, then leave the room.

An hour passes before Dad joins me in the kitchen. He sees the sandwich I've made for him and the glass of milk beside it. He eats the sandwich and gets up for a beer. After a moment I ask Dad if there is anything I can do for him. He barely moves his head.

"Did the nurse go home?" I question.

"I've asked her to stay," Dad answers. "I should have been here. She wanted me to be."

Dad is now talking about Mom, but he's got her sentiment wrong.

"I'm sorry you didn't get a chance to see her one more time," I say. I *am* sorry about this, but I'm not going to pretend Mom wanted him back. "You look awfully tired," I continue. "Let's go upstairs and I'll put some sheets on your bed while you watch the news."

Dad sits in a chair as I make his bed. I turn on the TV, and he stares at it. When I'm finished I ask Dad where his pajamas are. He motions toward his suitcase. I get them out for him and put them in his bathroom. I stay with Dad until he falls asleep, then turn the TV off and go to my room. Sleep is a relief, but in the morning I wake to face the unacceptable again.

I wander about the house and outside while people come and go, bringing food and offering their condolences. At one point in the day I disappear into the trunk room. When I emerge from hiding, I escape to the porch and watch the birds at the feeder. And sometime after sunset I wash a lot of strange dishes and go to bed.

The morning of the memorial service, Dad gets me out of bed to speak to Meg Benson on the phone. He tells me he's been up for hours and has had his breakfast. I know I'm not behaving as Dad wants me to, and I tell Meg on the phone that I'm a disappointment to him.

Later, Dad and I arrive at the church. Meg is in the vestibule, waiting for me. She looks strong. I want her to sit beside me in the church, but Dad sees to it that we sit alone in the first pew. The Bensons sit behind us.

I went to Sunday school in this church, was confirmed here, and sang in the choir one year. But knowing that Mom would not be welcome now because of who and how she loved, were it known, keeps me from feeling consoled. I stare at the white lilies on the chancel steps and remember how brilliant the sun was on Christmas Day when Mom and Gillian and I went for a walk, and Gillian kissed Mom in my presence.

After the services, in the church yard, I see Gillian standing alone. I try to loosen Dad's grip on my arm to go to her, but by the time I extricate myself, she is gone.

People are already at the house when Dad and I arrive. Dad joins the folks inside, and I go upstairs to Jeff's room. I don't come down for what could have been hours. Meg Benson finds me there and wakes me. She tells me she will stay with me if I would like. I shake my head, and she combs her fingers through my hair and says, "I loved your mother."

I'm not sure what she means. Does she mean that she, too, was in love with Mom? Or am I so confused I can't make good sense of anything?

In a fog, I get up and go downstairs with Meg. Chris and Ted and the others have gone. Bob is sitting with Dad. Dad is drinking something. I wish he weren't. Meg takes Dad's drink from him and offers to make everyone coffee. Dad looks up surprised but is too passive to complain. Like sheep, we follow Meg to the kitchen. Once there, in that most familiar setting, doing the ordinary, I begin to surface. It is as though my own photographic image were starting to appear on the paper.

The following day I take my camera and go to Setauket Beach. I don't ask Dad what his plans are nor invite him along with me. As I expected, Dad has found his place beside Jeff and seems content to remain there.

After shooting two rolls of film I get something to eat and go to a show. I don't come home until late, then creep up the stairs, hoping I won't wake Dad and have to answer for my absence.

My last morning at home begins with Dad asking if I will stay another week.

"I can't do that," I say.

"You're not going to drift away from us, are you?"

"Us?" I say.

"Jeff and me," Dad answers.

"No, Dad."

"When are we going to see you again?" he asks.

"I don't know, Dad. When I have some free time. I'd like to have Mom's car when it's fixed."

"I'll call you," Dad says.

"I'll see you then," I say.

"You blame me, don't you?" Dad says sadly.

"Blame you?" I ask surprised. "Why you? What for?"

"For everything."

"No, Dad, I don't blame you for everything. Why would I?"

"If I'd stayed home none of this would have happened."

A voice in me says don't do it, Bern, but I do. "That wouldn't have changed Mom and Gillian," I say.

"There was nothing to that," Dad answers sharply, and he gets up to pour himself a drink.

"If anything, that's what I blame," I say, staring at the bottle of scotch on the kitchen counter.

I go upstairs to pack my things. When I come down I hear music playing in the dining room. I could be generous, I think, and I start across the hall but stop at the closed door. Dad doesn't usually close the door. He's challenging me. I ache for him as well as myself, but I don't want to take care of him.

four

three years later

It's a warm day.
Dad is out back with
the garden hose, watering the
hostas that run along the porch, when
I come around the side of the house and surprise
him. He lifts his head and the hose and sprays me with
water. "Guess you weren't expecting anyone," I say. Dad drops the
hose and runs to me. We hug, then walk into the house together.

It is dark and cool inside and goose bumps rise under my wet
shirt. I pull away from Dad and hurry upstairs to change, then join
him minutes later on the porch.

It's been a year since I've seen him. For the first two years after
Mom died I came home for holidays and on an occasional weekend, but those were terrible times for me. Dad didn't want to talk
about Mom. I missed her, even more when I was at home. Within
a few hours of arriving I became gloomy, then irritable. Dad refused
to say why he wouldn't talk about her and didn't want me to. I was
left assuming that if I, who knew the truth about Mom, spoke of
her, he couldn't continue to deny her relationship with Gillian.

During my last visit, Dad was not merely sullen, but a pill for
four long weeks.

I had been printing in the darkroom when the hospital called to say my father had tripped on his back stairs, broken his right leg, and was a patient in the hospital. I hurried to his side.

The whole time I was with Dad at home he did nothing to take care of himself and complained about my care. Finally, one afternoon, I was so fed up with him that I walked out of the house and left him wondering if I would ever return.

That particular morning I had dragged myself out of bed to feed Jeff, change his diaper, and take Dad's breakfast up to him. Dad let me know that I was tardy, and I left his room without a word. Ordinarily, I would read to him when he finished breakfast. There was nothing wrong with Dad's eyesight. I'd made the mistake of reading to him his first day home from the hospital, and he expected me to continue thereafter. But that morning my eyes ached so in their sockets that I handed the newspaper to him. He wasn't interested enough to read to himself.

I went across the hall to my bathroom, took a couple aspirin, and laid down on my bed. I wasn't down fifteen minutes when Dad hollered out that he needed me. I pulled myself up, went to his room, and helped him to the bathroom.

By noon that day I'd bathed and shaved Jeff and made three trips to Dad's room to fetch him the telephone book from the library, a blueprint from his studio, and a glass of orange juice from the kitchen. I told Dad he would have to fend for himself after lunch and suggested he take a nice long nap so I could. But before I could fall asleep I heard him cry out. When I got to his room, I found Dad on the floor beside his bed.

"What on earth are you doing?" I asked.

"Fending for myself," he said.

"Not very well."

"What do you expect?"

"What is it this time, Dad?"

"You put my crutches too far away for me to reach them."

"I put them against the end table. You must have knocked them over."

"Of course I did. You put them too far away."

"Did you fall on the floor, Dad?"

"I sort of slid."

"Did you hurt yourself?"

"What do you care?"

I helped him up and asked him if he had to go to the bathroom.

"No."

"What is it then?"

"I want to go downstairs."

"You told me you didn't want to go down there."

"That was this morning. Now I do."

"All right, Dad, but then you're going to have to stay put. I can't help you in and out of rooms and on and off the porch today."

"I didn't ask you, did I?"

I helped Dad down the stairs, left him in the library, and went to speak to Jeff's nurse to ask if she would stay the rest of the day.

Within minutes of falling asleep a second time, I was awakened by a loud crash. I hurried downstairs, expecting to find Dad lying in a pool of blood. He was sitting in the chair where I'd left him but the wine decanter that had been on the table beside him was now broken on the floor in front of him.

"What happened?" I asked.

"I can't manage without her," he said.

"Without who?"

"Your mother."

"Well, you'll just have to find a way," I said.

"You don't have to make it worse," he answered.

"Make it worse! I'm running my butt off for you and I'm sick as a dog."

"I can't help it, Bern. I'm not used to being alone."

"You're not alone!" I shouted at him. I started to pick up the broken glass and stopped.

"Where're you going?" Dad asked as I started out of the room.

"I'm going out so you'll know just what it is to be alone."

I took my good time, returning to the house after dark. Dad was sitting at the kitchen table, crying over a bowl of Rice Krispies when I came in.

From then on I had an excuse every time Dad called to invite me for a weekend. After nearly a year, I got a letter from Dad with an apology. *I long to have your company,* he wrote, *to be with someone who knows me, even if what she knows is not all good. I'm sorry, Bern. Please come home for a visit and give me a chance to do better.*

Touched by Dad's plea, I went home.

On the porch, Dad hands me a drink. I take a gulp, not expecting a kick, and say, "I wish you would ask me if I want this stuff." Dad takes the drink from me and returns a moment later with a glass of plain lemonade.

In less than an hour Dad has had three tall glasses of spiked lemonade and is slouched down in his chair, looking bleak. Come to think of it, the surroundings look just as gloomy. In Mom's absence, the house has been neglected. The windows haven't been washed in three years, nor the curtains. Dad's beard is a couple days old and his hair is so long it curls at his neck. It's true I surprised him, but Dad used to be very careful about his appearance, shaving twice a day. I wonder how Jeff is doing and am surprised Dad hasn't asked me to go in and see him. When I ask Dad about his work, he tells me he's closed his office and is working full time at home. I know this. Dad never opened his office when he returned from England. It's the booze which has him confused. He's probably drinking more than ever these days, destroying countless brain cells with every ounce of liquor.

It's starting to happen. I'm starting to miss Mom. It always begins like this, watching Dad retreat into his dungeon of regret. I try to think of something cheerful, try not to embrace his lonesomeness, but it doesn't work.

"Where're you going," he asks when I stand.

"I'll be right back," I say.

In the bathroom I wash my face with cold water and wonder how she did it, how she managed not to succumb to his moods. Was she unaware? There were times when Mom didn't seem with us. In the end I forgave Mom her little absences. Why is it so hard to forgive Dad?

Dinner's been prepared. Dad just has to put it in the oven to warm it up, and he goes to the kitchen to do that while I remain in the library.

Over dinner Dad asks me how my work is going. I tell him I'm thinking of doing a book.

"What about?" he asks.

"About us," I say, wondering if I'll get an argument. Even before Gillian, Dad was a strong proponent of what-we-say-and-do-within-these-four-walls-remains-here.

Dad gets up from his chair and walks over to one of the bookshelves. "Ever read this?" he asks me, holding up Theodore Dreiser's *An American Tragedy*.

I answer, "Yes," but he knows that.

"Think you can write one as good?"

"I'm not writing a book," I explain.

"Your mom read this to me when I broke my arm."

"Dad, I read it to you when you broke your leg. Last summer.

Remember?"

"She was smarter than the bunch of us."

I nod my head in agreement with him, surprised he has brought her up.

"Too bad," he says, putting the book back on the shelf. I don't ask, *Too bad what?* Instead I tell Dad I'm doing a photography book, but I don't think he hears me. His eyes are fixed on something in his mind's eye. After a moment he asks, "Why are you writing about us?"

"I'm not writing a book, Dad. I'm a photographer, remember?" Dad doesn't seem embarrassed that he needs to be reminded of this, nor does he seem annoyed at me. I suggest we go in and see Jeff. He gets up.

Jeff's hair and beard are as long as Dad's.

"Have you been doing the range of motion exercises?" I ask, and Dad nods his head.

"What about the nurse?"

He nods again.

"How often does she come?" I ask, aspirating the nasogastric tube to see if Jeff has digested his last meal, then filling the bag with Sustacal. Dad sits beside Jeff. Instead of answering my question, he tells Jeff I'm home on a visit and that I'm planning to put together a photography book about the family.

"Jeff will be in it, won't he?" Dad asks me.

"Of course," I answer. I step over to the tape recorder and put something on. Jeff makes a face. It's an involuntary response to the feeding activity. Jeff doesn't know he's eating. His body knows, but he doesn't.

When the bag is empty I fill a syringe with water and irrigate the feeding tube. Jeff's head must remain up for at least a half hour so he will not aspirate his dinner.

Dad and I sit quietly with him. Finally, I ask, "When did you bathe him last?"

"Yesterday."

"Any sore spots?"

"No."

We are quiet again for several minutes before Dad offers to change Jeff's diaper. He would be ill at ease doing that with me present, so I kiss Jeff on the cheek and leave the room.

The next day I'm up at seven. By nine the kitchen counter is cluttered with every glass object that isn't a fixture of the house—figurines, ashtrays, paperweights, candle holders, coasters, flower vases, and lamp chimneys—and I've got a sink full of ammonia water. Dad's been up since five and is in with Jeff. When I'm done here I plan to call a window washer and the cleaners to give me an estimate on cleaning the upholstery and curtains. Dad thinks all this is unnecessary.

After finishing my work in the kitchen I go to the library, make my calls, then get down the family photo albums and settle in on a patch of sunlight on the floor to pore over them.

Dad interrupts me as I'm looking at a picture of Mom, sitting in an easy chair with her feet up on an ottoman. In it, she's wearing a chenille robe over pajamas and reading a magazine. She can't be more than twenty-five in the snapshot. Her hair is to her shoulders, her face fuller than I remember it.

"I found something that might interest you," Dad says. He hands me a photo of himself as a young man. In it he is standing with his arm around a woman I don't recognize.

"Who is she?" I ask.

"Doris Spalding."

"Were you lovers?" I ask.

"We were sweethearts," he says.

"Where was this picture?" I ask.

Dad doesn't answer. He has his hand out, waiting for me to pass it back to him. I hand over the picture, and Dad runs away.

A half hour later he's back with something else to show me. It's a worn photo of Dad as a young boy with one of those dogs that Spanky and His Gang had.

"Whose dog?" I ask.

"Mine," Dad says. "You know, Patches?"

"No, I don't."

"You sure?"

"I'm sure," I say.

When Jeff was in grade school he tried to talk Mom and Dad into allowing him to have a dog. Dad said that if we had a dog we would show it the affection we ought to show one another, and we didn't get one.

"He used to follow me to school," Dad says. "And wait on the doorstep all day."

"He stayed there all day?" I ask, amazed.

"If he had an adventure or two, I didn't know about it. He was always there, waiting for me when the bell rang." Dad looks at the photo fondly. "I was kind of a solitary kid," he says. "Patches and I went on imaginary adventures together. Maybe that's why I didn't tell you about him. Maybe I thought I'd made him up."

"Where was this picture?" I ask.

"In an old wallet of mine," Dad answers. "I sure loved that dog," he says sweetly.

"Why don't you get one now?"

"No," Dad answers, putting the picture in his back pocket.

"Be nice for you to have a dog."

"I have Jeff," Dad says, patting his back pocket.

"Can I borrow the photograph to make a print for myself?"

Reluctantly Dad gives the picture to me, then gets down on the floor beside me. He turns a page in the photo album and almost touches a picture of Mom on her bike up at the cabin. His hand approaches, then retreats from it, and I wonder how long before I mess with his memory, with his version of how things were, and this sweetness turns sour?

Dad flips the page and pauses, this time to look at a picture of our young family on a Nantucket beach. It doesn't show in the picture, but I have a wad of cotton in one of my ears. I remember the week we spent at the Rooneys' cottage I had an ear ache and was miserable because I couldn't go swimming.

On the same page is a picture of Dad with a drink in one hand and a cigarette in the other. In a good number of pictures Dad has a drink, but in only a few is he smoking.

"When'd you stop smoking?" I ask.

"When you were kids," he says. "I got the Asian flu and lost my desire."

"Is there anything that could make you lose your desire for a drink?" I ask.

"Nothing has," Dad answers cheerfully.

"Mom ever ask you to quit?"

"You're not going to lecture me about my drinking, are you?"

"There'd be little point in that," I say, turning the page. Dad says he's hungry and stands up. I agree and join him on the porch minutes later.

Over lunch Dad tells me he would like to go sailing the next day. I give him a nod, but I'm not paying attention. I'm thinking about Dad and Doris and wondering why he showed me the photo of them.

That evening I cut first Jeff's, then Dad's, hair. "Should we take lunch out with us?" Dad asks. He's sitting on a bar stool in the kitchen with a sheet wrapped around his shoulders.

"Out?" I say, then remember. "Oh, sailing. Yeah, I'll make us sandwiches before I go to bed."

"I can do that," he answers. "You've done enough today."

"Yeah, but you'll make peanut butter and jelly," I say, kidding him. One of the photos in the album I'd asked Dad about was a picture of him on a donkey going into the Grand Canyon. All Dad could remember of the trip was that he had taken two peanut butter sandwiches and a canteen of water on the journey with him, drank all the water before he ate the sandwiches, and then had nothing to wash down the peanut butter.

The next day, in the station wagon on the way to the yacht club, I tell Dad I'd rather take the Turncoat out. The Turncoat is a cabin cruiser. I remembered Dad reporting to me in a recent letter that he and Ted Rooney were sailing in the Sound when something or other happened and the Coast Guard had to bring them in.

"Why's that?" Dad asks me.

"I don't feel like crewing," I say. "I'd rather take it easy."

"I'm sure we can get someone to crew for us," Dad offers.

"I'd rather be alone with you," I respond.

Dad takes his eyes off the road ahead to look at me beside him. This is just great, I think. While I worry about an accident on the high seas we'll run off the road.

"All right, honey. We can take the Turncoat out and go sailing another day."

I nearly sigh out loud as I relax back against the car seat.

By eleven o'clock Dad and I are pulling away from the dock. I sit up on the foredeck and enjoy the wind in my face and the smell of sea water and deck varnish. The water's surface is dancing with sunlight, and I can't look at it without squinting. Once we are out of the harbor I climb back to have coffee and eat a sandwich with

Dad. He's got his canvas boat hat so far down on his forehead that I can't see his eyes. I turn the brim up. He gives me a goofy smile, so I get my camera and take a roll of film of him.

I don't think there's anything in the world that makes Dad happier than being on a boat with his family. Although my folks had an active social life, I always knew they preferred their private lives—Dad on a boat with his family and Mom up at the cabin with one of us or alone.

After we've been out for the better part of an hour and relatively quiet, I ask Dad why he continues to hold onto Jeff.

"He's my son," Dad says, looking surprised by my question.

"Is he really?" I ask. "Isn't he just the body of your son?" Dad doesn't like the question and doesn't answer me. "Is Jeff in his body?" I push.

"I don't know, Bern."

"You must think he is. Why do you?"

"Why do you want to know what I think?"

"Because."

"Because why?"

"Because I'm not sure what life is and I'd like to be. I'd like to know for sure if Jeff is alive."

"He is," Dad says, and I challenge him.

"Tell me how his body is any different than a well-cared for organ being preserved for a transplant?"

"I don't know how you can say such things," Dad says to shut me up.

"But you do know why you hold on to him," I answer.

"I told you why."

"I think there's more to it. Is it guilt? Do you feel responsible because you were in the boat with him?"

"That's enough, Bern. I don't want to talk about this any more."

"Why?"

Dad refuses to answer me. I've gained the upper hand and I can't resist pushing him further.

"Were you responsible, Dad?" I see the color drain from Dad's face. "Why do you feel you're responsible?"

"Stop it. Now!"

"Was it you? It was you, wasn't it? You were driving the boat. It's always seemed strange to me that Jeff hit the rocks. It was you, wasn't it?"

Dad shakes his head, but I know better by the look in his eyes.

It is a hollow victory for me. I try to put my arm around him. He won't let me. I say I'm sorry, but it's too late to be sorry. "I did it because I'm mad at you," I say. "Because you always retreat into the bottle when things get difficult for you."

"I should have been the one to die," Dad says. He's crying.

Die? According to Dad, Jeff wasn't dead. Holding on hadn't kept Jeff alive to Dad anymore than he was to Mom and me.

After a moment I say, "It doesn't matter who was driving. It's the same tragedy." I know full well it is not the same tragedy, that my father has never been able to forgive himself and move forward since that July Fourth weekend because he was driving the boat.

That day, like all days, Dad had been drinking. Looking at him now, broken in spirit, I don't feel angry with him. I feel sorry for him. I see so clearly that he cannot stop punishing himself. And to dull the pain he continues to drink. This time when I put my arm around him he doesn't pull away. "I'm sorry," I say.

"I asked your mom to marry me on a day like this," Dad says, changing the subject.

"Tell me about that."

"We were out here sailing."

I can imagine Mom thinking Dad was topnotch. He was handsome and refined and already a successful marine architect.

"Before she said yes she made me promise some things. In particular I had to promise her she wouldn't have to socialize with people who bored her. It would be fine if I did, but she wouldn't pretend to be interested in the details afterward and probably wouldn't ask." Dad turns and looks at me. "It was an easy promise to make. She's all I ever wanted."

This makes me sad. I'm sad for Dad because he didn't desire more, and sad for Mom because she had the burden of being everything to him.

"Jean always interested me more than I interested her," Dad says looking past me.

"She married you," I say.

"She did that," he says sadly, then turns the Yankees-Orioles game on the radio. I return to the foredeck as we cross the Sound to Bridgeport. I can hear the game as I fall off to sleep. When I wake we are just leaving the Connecticut harbor. My skin feels tight, so I crawl back to Dad and get out of the sun. Dad says he picked something up for me in Bridgeport and hands me an old soggy sock he's fished out of the harbor.

"Guess you wish you'd had this to stuff in my mouth an hour ago," I say, smiling.

The rest of the way back to the yacht club I sit beside Dad. We don't talk, but I feel forgiven. My heart aches for him. I am sorry, and I wish he believed that. It could have been any one of us driving the boat. We have all been careless, but to say so wouldn't help.

The next day I come down for breakfast prepared to tell Dad that I forgive him. I notice the door to the trunk room is open and I look in. Dad is sitting on the floor, his pinstripe pajama top tucked into a pair of corduroys, with his wedding album open on his lap. A streak of light coming from the hallway provides him with just enough light to see by. Unnoticed, I slip away to get my camera. When Dad hears the shutter click he looks up. "I didn't know you were there," he says.

I negotiate around trunks, suitcases, and cardboard boxes to the darkest recess of the trunk room and turn on a light.

"Where'd that come from?" he asks.

I invite Dad over to my cubbyhole. He steps over a rolled rug and loses a slipper. "Well, I'll be," he says when he sees the sleeping bag nestled between two steamer trunks. "Pretty snazzy. Where's the light hooked up?" he asks.

I show Dad the hole I drilled years ago which goes through the wall to the hallway where there's a wall plug.

"That's smart of you," he says.

"Gee, Dad, if I'd known you'd be impressed I'd have shown it to you years ago."

"Guess what I found, Bern?"

"Your wedding album," I say.

"My Louisville Slugger," he says, and Dad points to a barrel which holds rolls of wallpaper, window shades, and his baseball bat. "There are probably other things in here I had as a kid," he says hopefully.

"I'll bet there are, Dad."

Dad unrolls a foot of white-and-yellow Victorian wallpaper which is quite beautiful and brittle with age. "This used to be in the hallway upstairs," he says. Next, Dad lifts the top of a steamer trunk. "Close your eyes, Bern."

I do as he says, and a moment later he tells me I can open them.

Behold, Dad is holding up my bunny costume, which is every bit as wonderful as I remember it. "There must be a picture of you in this somewhere," he says, as he puts the Halloween costume down and takes something else out of the trunk. It's a large Bergdorf Goodman box which contains Mom's wedding dress. Jeff and I used to open the box and marvel at it, never touching it because that would have been sacrilege. We were in awe of our idea of Mom as a bride.

Dad takes the box over to the door, I think to have a better look. Instead, he leaves with it. Since neither Jeff nor I ever took the dress out of the box, I don't know if there is anything else, something Dad may want to remove in private. Or if Dad just wants to be alone with the dress and his memories.

My first visit home after Mom died I woke in the middle of the night to go to the bathroom. From there I could hear Dad in the guest room. The next day when I asked Dad what he had been doing in Mom's room, he denied having been there. Why was Dad shy about saying he went to Mom's room to be with her? I was never shy about telling anyone I went to Jeff's room for that purpose. I even reported things I was sure Jeff told me on my visits.

Among the boxes and trunks and suitcases I don't recall anyone ever using are stacks of books and old phonograph albums, picture frames, my hamster cage, camping gear, a couple of old doors, and a standing mirror.

When Dad returns to the room I ask him whatever happened to the trunk of shoes. He tells me that Mom gave them away to the Salvation Army on one of her cleaning sprees.

"Too bad," I say. "They'd probably be in fashion again."

Dad's intent on finding something. When he does he hollers out, "Got it!"

"What?!" I ask, excited.

"My scrapbook," he says, and he hurries out of the trunk room with it. This time I follow Dad and take a picture of him sitting on the floor in the hall, leaning against the stair wall, with the scrapbook open on his lap and a smile on his face. He is in his glory, remembering his youth and looking younger, suddenly. I love my dad like this, happy with himself.

Before leaving the trunk room I straighten it up. As I'm putting things away I remember a box of letters, and after searching through several trunks, I find the small box among some miscellaneous items. Inside are Dad's love letters to Mom. I take the bundle out of the box, pull my shirt tail out of my shorts so I can tuck them under my waistband, and sneak out of the house.

The afternoon sun is hot. I climb down the cliff steps to the water's edge and sit with my feet in the cool water to read the letters. Jeff and I used to pore over them when we were kids, not understanding half of what we read. My father was quite the romantic, writing sonnets to Mom. When I return to the house, an hour later, Dad is gone. He's left me a note telling me he's at the club, asking me to join him. I shower and change my clothes. On my way over, though, I think better of it and drive by a high school hangout, then every familiar landmark of my youth, winding my way to Mattituck where I get a sandwich from a deli and continue on to Greenport. Dad's love letters have made me think of Gillian.

Dad's with Jeff when I get in. I tell him where I've been and that I'm going to bed. He doesn't challenge me when I say I didn't see his note.

My last morning at home I hear Dad overhead and go up to see him before breakfast. He is seated at his large work table under the skylight.

"Whatcha doing?" I ask, eyeing the blueprint in front of Dad.

"Nothing you'd understand," he says, sounding annoyed. Is he suffering from a hangover? I wonder.

"Remember when I put goldfish in here?" I say, pretending I haven't noticed his sour mood.

Dad looks up at me, standing beside the large tank where he used to float his prototypes. For years there's been no water in it.

"Of course I remember that," he says.

"Am I bothering you?" I ask.

Dad returns to his blueprint and says nothing for what seems a long while. Then, without looking up, he asks me if I'm going to have any photos of "that woman" in my book?

"Gillian Eames?" I ask, and when Dad doesn't answer I say, "Yes, she's a part of it. She was a part of Mom's life."

"Why do you feel it necessary to embarrass me?" he asks.

"Why is she embarrassing?" I answer.

"You know why!"

"I hope to show each of us truthfully, Dad. I don't think the truth will shame anyone."

"If you want to bare your ass, that's fine, but you have no right to make an exhibition of others."

I don't recall my dad ever being so blunt. I'm shocked and more than a little afraid of him. "What will you do?" I ask.

"Ache for us all," he answers.

"What changed your mind?" I ask. "All weekend you've supported the idea of a book about us."

"I was foolish enough to think when you said family you meant the four of us."

"We haven't lived isolated lives. Photos like the one of you and Patches and you and Doris are important. They show your humanity, Dad."

"Where is your humanity?" he asks.

I look down at the empty tank. I don't think Dad actually needed the tank to test his models. He built it for Jeff and me to play with when we visited him in his studio. We must have distracted him at times, but he never made us feel unwelcome. I took his generosity for granted, and now I have pushed it to its limit. Do I have a moral right to reveal the truth about my family? What can any artist offer but herself? And how can she do that without involving others? But family and friends do pay a price.

I left home that day as I often did—confused. Had it been a good visit or not? Was I right or wrong to say what I said and do what I intended to do? Would Dad ever speak to me again? Would I want to speak to him? On whose terms?

five

With six fam-
ily albums in the trunk
of the Citroen, I drive into the
Midtown Tunnel, the place where concerns about my family are usually over-
shadowed by the pressures of my work. But today I can't
get Dad out of my mind. I can't forget that he is the only family I
have and I have hurt him. He would be surprised to know it bothers
me so.

Several messages are waiting for me on my answer phone. The
stock house called to say they sold a picture, *Esquire* called to ask
where the Bronx Ball pictures are, and Sam Something—I don't
catch his last name—called to say he will pick me up at seven. Sam
is a friend of friends, and my blind date for the night.

I take a shower, dress, and hand deliver the Bronx Ball prints
to the art director at *Esquire*. Bronx Ball is a game the kids play in
the streets, which, unlike a generation earlier, now includes girls. The
art director knows nothing about a rush for the prints, but says the
editor has a bug up his ass about the summer sloth.

At home in my apartment, I wish I hadn't accepted a date. I
don't feel like going out again. I'd rather set up my camera and sit
up all night, photographing pictures from the family albums. I want
to go back, look it all over again, and find the part I played.

Dressed in a summer skirt and blouse, waiting for the last min-ute to put on sandals, I go to the phone and call Gillian. I haven't spoken to her in three years, although we have exchanged Christmas cards. I've thought of her often, been curious about her, and won-dered if she had adjusted to the loss of Mom.

Gillian doesn't sound surprised to hear from me, nor reluctant to see me. She suggests I come out on Monday because the first days of the week are slow for her. She asks if I still have the directions and reminds me to take the north ferry. With her on my mind all night, I go to a show and to dinner afterward with Sam. In the dark of the theater I'm reminded of Mom and me in that small movie house up at the cabin, being shushed by the woman behind us for whispering about Gillian.

Monday morning, bright and early, I leave the city. It's a hot day, and the Citroen's air conditioner is on the fritz. The car is in the shop more than in the parking garage. I know a car that's been in a head-on collision is a poor risk, but I had to take it up, just as I had had to take up Jeff's camera.

Three hours later I get out of the car for the ferry ride. The breeze off the Bay blows against my wet shirt, and I actually feel chilled. On the road again, I'm nervous. I invited myself and won-der if that was wise. This visit may not be the best thing for me or her. What if we are awkward with one another?

Just beyond the farm stand I turn up a gravel drive. If it were possible at this point to retreat I might but, rumbling over gravel and kicking up a cloud of dust, I announce my arrival. Gillian is waiting for me on the front porch of the large, gray clapboard farm-house. The instant I see her I'm glad that I'm here.

"It's about time!" she hollers out as she jumps off the porch and hurries to the car. With her arm around me, Gillian takes me into her house, down a center hall, to the kitchen, a big room with white cupboards and a black-and-white linoleum floor. An orange cat is stretched out in a patch of sunlight on the floor, an ironing board is set up in the middle of the room, and laundry is heaped up on the kitchen table and chairs.

"Have a seat there," Gillian says, pointing to a chair. "Just push that stuff aside."

I take the things off the chair, add them to the pile on the table, and sit down.

"Which would you rather, tea or coffee?"

"Either one," I say.

Gillian brings me a glass of iced tea, sets it down on the edge of the table, and tosses the clothes on the table into a laundry basket on the floor. "I couldn't sleep last night," she explains, "so I got up and ironed." The kitchen smells like scorched cotton, and shirts hang from every cupboard knob. "I usually go out and putter in the greenhouse when I'm restless, but I asked one of my workers to take care of things for me so I could be with you. He did such a good job of it there wasn't anything left for me to do. How are you, Bern?"

"I didn't sleep much last night, either," I say.

"And the drive out was probably beastly. It always is in the summer."

"It wouldn't have been bad if I'd had some air conditioning."

"How is the car?"

"Not what she used to be," I say.

Gillian removes laundry from the chair opposite me and sits down. "I went to your show," she says. "Not the opening, as you know. I thought my appearance that night might put a damper on things."

"Yes, thank you, I saw your name in the book."

"What are you doing now?"

"Same stuff. How are you doing?" I ask.

Gillian smiles and says, "I'll show you in a moment. Have you been home recently?" she asks.

"Yes, just."

"How was it?"

"Hard, as always."

"How so?" Gillian asks.

"Dad is mad at me." Gillian looks interested, and I go on. "We've always had trouble."

"I'm sorry," she says.

I think about not saying anymore, but do, saying things I've never said to anyone. "He drinks too much, always has, and I resent it. Every visit we end up bickering about something. When Dad is passive I become aggressive and mean in response."

Gillian remains quiet.

"He sits beside Jeff for hours...holding on out of loneliness and guilt. I got him to admit he was to blame."

Gillian looks at me curiously.

"It was Dad who crashed the boat on the rocks. I don't think Mom ever knew, but she might have guessed it. Did she ever say anything to you about it?"

"No."

"I wish now I hadn't pushed Dad," I say, but Gillian disagrees. I'm not sure what she means by shaking her head so I ask her.

"You shouldn't punish yourself for wanting to know the truth."

I'm not sure I agree with her.

"I was so excited, thrilled, you could even say, when Mom and Dad brought Jeff home from the hospital. It had been weeks but it felt like months. Jeff and I had been close. I missed him.... It might have been different if he'd been the older one. Boys don't like their baby sisters hanging around them. Jeff was my best friend. I liked doing things with him—boy things."

Gillian smiles, and I want to go on.

"He looked normal when he came home from the hospital, except his head was bandaged, and he was in a kind of trance. Every day I'd wake with renewed hope that when I went to see Jeff he would be back, returned to me. It was hard to see he wasn't. I don't know why I'm telling you all this," I say, and I go on.

"After a year of hoping and praying and being disappointed over and over again, I gave up. I stopped going into the dining room to see Jeff. I sought his company upstairs, through my memory and in my imagination. At first Mom and Dad didn't notice. I shouldn't be mad at Dad for escaping into his fantasy because I know all about it.

Gillian reaches across the table to take my hand in hers.

"There is no escaping the truth," I say. "And Dad knows that, too. I take pictures in an attempt to make friends with the truth because I know I can't escape it."

"Yes," Gillian says, "but the people you photograph always appear brave. If not happy, at least not angry at their circumstances. What about that? Do you think we shouldn't be angry at life?"

I shrug my shoulders, which is as good as saying I do.

"You have good reason to be angry, Bern."

"I don't know about that," I say, and Gillian lets go of my hand.

"How was it being an exile?" she asks.

"What do you mean?"

"In your brother's room, upstairs."

"Lonely."

"You must have been angry at your mother and father for allowing you to slip away?"

"I missed them. But they were busy. In the beginning Mom did everything she could think of to arouse Jeff. She worked with him day and night, never letting up, and rarely sleeping through a night.

It was a lot of years before she did something nice for herself," I say, looking directly at Gillian.

"Do you suppose you needed your mother and father to be happy survivors in order for you to be that?" Gillian asks.

"Maybe," I answer.

"And that's why you're more angry with your father?"

"Probably," I say.

"And maybe you're too quick to defend your mother. She was your mother too, not just Jeff's, and she let you down."

I don't argue with Gillian, but neither do I agree with her. After a moment I say, "It's hard sometimes to think of her dead," and Gillian nods her head.

"She was so full of life, such a fighter. Jeff got his adventurous spirit from Mom. I'm cautious like Dad." Gillian looks unconvinced. Instead of providing proof of my shortcomings, I go on about Mom.

"Nothing was too much for her. Did you know in the beginning she used to feed Jeff by hand, putting the food way back on his tongue until he gagged and swallowed? It was difficult to do, and painful to watch."

"Bern, I know you feel your brother was the photographer and you came by it accidently, but I wonder if you aren't the one who sees things."

It had never been suggested to me that I was a natural at photography, and I'm surprised, but pleasantly, by her compliment.

"And you're more like your mother than you give yourself credit for," Gillian says. "You weren't cautious in accepting your mother and me."

"It took me three years to come here," I say.

"Someone else might never have."

I give Gillian a look that now she's being too generous, and she asks me if I would like to see the house.

The downstairs rooms are large and square and crowded with a hodgepodge of furniture, odds and ends, and photographs. Floral printed slipcovers from another era cover the chairs and sofas. And large windows let in great streams of sunlight, making the rooms, which could otherwise seem dreary, cheerful.

Gillian walks from room to room, carrying the shirts she's ironed, and moving with a sort of graceful purpose that I think is particular to women.

After I've seen the downstairs we start up the stairs to the second floor. The steps, worn from wear, dip in the middle and form a hollowed pathway upward. For a brief moment in the stairwell, I slip outside myself and imagine I'm Mom, seeing the house for the first time. What did Mom think? I wonder. And know that she loved it for its lived-in quality.

Three bedrooms and a study are on the second floor. Instead of continuing up to the third floor, Gillian and I return downstairs and go out for a walk, pass the greenhouse to the cutting garden. I take my camera along and photograph the daylilies. Gillian snips off a bouquet of dahlias and hands them to me.

At the vegetable garden Gillian bends down to pull out a weed, and seeing others, crouches to get them. I watch and wonder how things might have been different for me if I'd come out here right after Mom died. Maybe this place would have been a comfort to me.

"This is my therapy," Gillian says, looking up at me from a row of squash.

"Did you have a hard time?" I ask.

"I did," Gillian says, standing and shaking clods of dirt from a handful of weeds she's holding.

"You seem so strong," I say, and Gillian doesn't answer.

While Gillian goes to check on the farm stand and close up shop, I find a vase for the dahlias, then take my Nikon, which has a roll of color film in it, back to the gardens to shoot pictures for myself. I walk along row upon row of perennials and vegetables which cover half an acre and must require an enormous amount of time and energy to maintain, and I think about Mom plowing these rows. Before going back to the house, I visit the greenhouse where plants of every variety are nurtured. I can identify only a few. I didn't inherit my mother's green thumb, but I do delight in the exotic beauty and the smell of the damp earth. They remind me of a summer's day after a rainstorm. It is easy to understand the appeal of this work.

I return to the house and sit down in the living room. Sometime later, Gillian wakes me from my nap on the sofa to tell me supper's ready. I'm embarrassed that I fell asleep and didn't offer to help her with the preparations.

Compared to the other rooms, the dining room is plain. I ask Gillian why that is, and she tells me decorations would steal attention from the cuisine. I can't tell if she's serious or poking fun at her meal which is delicious but presented informally: grilled chicken breasts on a chipped platter and braised potatoes, onions, peppers, and squash from her garden in bowls as old and worn.

Gillian tells me her grandfather made the long pine table we are seated at, although he was a botanist, not a carpenter, and her grandmother was a schoolteacher. I realize, as she speaks about them, that I know nothing about Gillian's parents.

"My grandparents raised me," she says. "I thought you knew that."

"No, I didn't."

"I was born out of wedlock. My mother and I lived here with them until my mother met and married a man from Texas. I didn't want to move west with them so I stayed here with my grandparents. I didn't like my stepfather, and I loved my grandparents and this place."

"Did you feel abandoned by your mother?"

"You know, Bern, I never felt she was my mother. She was only fifteen when I was born."

"Is she still in Texas?"

"Yes, they are. They have a family down there. I have a half brother and two half sisters."

"Do you ever see them?"

"Every couple years or so I go down."

"Is it strange?"

"Yes, it is," Gillian says, and I sigh.

Gillian asks me what the sigh was about and I ask her, "Do you think there is such a thing as the all-American family?"

Gillian almost laughs and says, "Yes, yours and mine."

In a sudden wave of sadness, I tell Gillian we don't talk about Mom at home.

"You can talk to me about her," she says, and she puts down her fork to listen.

"I stopped going home because Dad wouldn't let me talk about Mom. He lies to himself about her and wants me to go along with it."

"I'm sorry, Bern."

"I miss her so."

"I know," Gillian says.

"Is this too painful?" I ask.

"Not too painful," she says, then adds, "I haven't talked much about her either."

Gillian and I resume eating. After several moments I ask her what she thought of Mom being married, and she says, "I was concerned your parents' history would hold them together and keep Jean from being with me."

"Did you ever worry that she might be experimenting with

you?"

"No, I didn't feel that."

"The day she died—" I say, then stop myself.

"I didn't tell you much about that because you didn't ask," Gillian says. "I don't know how much the hospital or police told you."

"Just that the guy who hit her was drunk and ran from the scene. He left his disabled truck which is how they identified him. I don't want to know his name or what happened to him."

Gillian nods her head then takes a moment before saying, "Jean was late arriving that evening, so I called Old Field, and your brother's nurse told me she'd left hours before. I got in my car and drove over to the ferry expecting to find something was holding it up. But nothing was, so I took it across the Bay and headed toward Old Field. I kept telling myself it was probably something silly like a flat tire or an empty gas tank, but I was shaking the whole time.

"I saw the truck first. It didn't look badly damaged, but apparently its front wheel was broken. Jean's car was on the other side of the road. . . are you sure you want to hear this?"

I'm not sure, but I don't say anything.

"Your mother's car was smashed in on the driver's side, front and side. I wasn't able to open her door. I got her out from the passenger side."

"Was anyone else there?" I ask.

"No, and I don't know why because it's a busy road. People must have passed by without noticing Jean or not wanting to get involved. I stopped someone and asked them to call an ambulance. But your mom was already dead. Her chest had been crushed."

"Oh, god, how horrible for you."

"At that point, Bern, it wasn't as horrible as you might think. I was in shock. I have flashes of me struggling to get Jean out of the car, and holding her on the side of the road with car lights shining on us."

"Did you go to the hospital with her?"

Gillian nods her head. I can tell by her expression that this is very painful to recall. "You don't have to tell me any more," I say, but she goes on.

"We were separated at the hospital, and I was given something to calm me down. I telephoned a friend of mine who lives on the Island and she came."

"Where did they take Mom?"

"They didn't tell me. But they did tell my friend, Judy, that she was dead on arrival and was being held at the hospital while they tried to locate her family. I didn't know how to reach your father, but I thought Jeff's nurse might, so I gave them the Old Field number.

"Judy took me home with her. I called you from her place the next morning. I should have given Judy your number to call that night, but for some reason I didn't."

"I'm glad it was you who called," I say.

"I worried you might be upset with me for not phoning you immediately."

"No, it never occurred to me to question that. I felt you called me as soon as you could."

"I went over to Old Field that day."

"To remove all evidence of yourself in the house," I say, and Gillian nods her head.

"I didn't want your father coming home and having to deal with that, too."

"I tried to get away from him after the service to talk to you. Everyone was saying how sorry they were for us, and there you were, standing all by yourself."

"You know what that's like, don't you?" Gillian says, and I get up from my seat at the table and go to her. I lean down and she reaches up and we hug one another. It's awkward because I'm standing and she's sitting. We are so uncoordinated in our gesture that we are forced to laugh through our tears.

Gillian and I clear the table and return to the dining room for coffee. I ask her how she got over the pain, and she says, "I lived with it, and eventually some joy returned to my life, filling in the sad, empty places. . . . Isn't that what happened to you?" she asks.

"I don't think I've been as willing as you to let joy in."

"Each in her own time," Gillian says. "You can't hurry nature."

"Do you trust the universe that much?" I ask, and Gillian answers brightly, "I *am* a gardener."

We finish our coffee and go out to get my bags from the car. I follow her up the stairs. She takes me to a small room which has a crib on rockers full of old magazines, a side chair, and a narrow bed with a pillow and a quilt.

"There's no chest of drawers or closet in here," Gillian says, "but it was Jean's favorite."

"Yes," I answer. "I'd like to stay here."

"There's a bathroom next door."

We say good night and Gillian leaves. When she's gone I turn off the light in the room and pull the chair over to the window, take a deep breath of night air, and wonder where Mom is tonight, if she knows where I am.

Dawn of the following day Gillian nudges me awake. "Get up!" she says excitedly. "We're going over to the Yeager's to see some puppies."

"Puppies?" I ask.

"Yes, come on!"

Gillian hurries out of my room. She's kidding, I think. It can't be seven o'clock. I close my eyes, but she yells up the stairs to me once more and I'm forced to get up.

Half awake, I join Gillian in the kitchen. She has on a garden-ing smock and has been up for hours, looking after things. She hands me a cardigan sweater of Mom's to put on. We step outside into the damp morning.

Mabel Yeager, a stocky woman with dark curly hair, leads us into her pantry. The two puppies and their mother are asleep in one half of an old suitcase below a pantry shelf of fruit preserves. Gil-lian puts her arm around me and squeezes me as I think she would like to squeeze the puppies. Then, sensing some shyness in me, she declines Mabel's invitation to stay for biscuits. We are given a nap-kinful to take home with us.

"Did Mabel know about you and Mom?" I ask Gillian as we cut across the tennis court.

"Yes, your mother told her. They ran into one another before I could introduce them. Mabel asked Jean if she was a friend of mine, and your mother said, point-blank, that she was my lover."

"Mom said that?!"

"Mabel likes to put people on the spot, to give herself an edge. It didn't work with Jean."

"How did she put Mom on the spot?"

"I think it was the way she said *friend*."

Gillian and I step inside the farmhouse, and I start to remove Mom's sweater. When she asks me if I'd like to have it, I put my arm back in the sleeve and my hands in the pockets. I feel something in one of the pockets and pull it out. It's a packet of chicory seeds. A moment later the phone rings, and I leave the kitchen to give Gillian some privacy.

"That was a friend," she says when I return. "She's coming out for a few days."

Gillian looks relieved that I don't ask her about the friend. Instead I ask Gillian what she and Mom did on the Island.

"We putzed around here," she says, "and went for walks. Hey, would you like to go down to the harbor?"

As Gillian washes, I dry our breakfast dishes. She doesn't seem to care where I put them. When I ask her what cupboard they go in, she says any will do.

An hour later we get in her car and take the Shore Road to the harbor. After buying clams for our supper we sit on the pier with our legs dangling over the side and share a soda. I tell Gillian I'm going to put together a photography book of family pictures and ask her if she minds being in it.

"Dad minds, of course. He thinks I'm doing it just to embarrass him. What about you?" I ask.

"No, I don't mind."

"What about telling the truth about my family? Do you think I should?"

"There's a price to be paid for being open, even in a society that's supposed to be free like ours. What price are you willing to pay?"

"And what price am I willing to make Dad pay?" I say.

"You haven't the right to demand he reveal himself to anyone. But neither has he the right to stop you from revealing the truth about your mom."

"Does that mean you're in favor of outing someone?"

"Under some circumstances."

"When aren't you?" I ask, and Gillian says, "Motive counts."

"How do you feel about people in the closet?" I ask.

"I don't recommend it," she says. "The truth is easier. It ought to be the one thing we all have access to and defend, but it isn't. That's why art is so important."

"I don't think Dad would call my baring the family's ass art."

Gillian laughs, then says, "Your father could surprise you. He hasn't seen your book. He only imagines it in the worst possible way. You'll do your best, and he'll either be honored by it or ashamed. That will be his choice."

"He didn't like me using Mom in *Missing Parts*. He never said so, but I feel certain he thought I exploited her. He thinks I should stick to embarrassing myself."

"What are you going to do, Bern?"

"Well, there's a photo of me as a chubby adolescent with acne. I'm naked, floating in an inner tube up at the lake, and you can count the rolls around my belly."

"That's good," Gillian says, laughing.

"Would you like to know the photo of you I'm thinking of using?" I ask, and Gillian's smile fades. I tell her she can relax, she's the most photogenic of the lot.

"About that picture of you," she says, teasing me—

"I'd be happy to send you a print to hang with all those you have in your living room."

"That would be nice," she says.

Gillian puts her arm around my shoulder when we get up and we walk to the car. I feel a need to make it clear how I feel about Mom and her love.

"Gillian, about Mom and you. *I'm* not ashamed. And I'm not doing this to shock anyone either. It's what I do, show the human behind the face. I only want to show my family's human face."

"You don't need to defend yourself Bern. I'm all for it."

Before pulling into the drive we stop at the farm stand, and Gillian gets out of the car to talk to the young woman who manages it for her.

Gillian stands with one hand tucked under the waistband of her shorts, supporting her back, and the other shielding her eyes from the sun. Her arms and legs are strong and suntanned from the work she does. She's old enough to be the other woman's mother but doesn't look it. When Gillian lowers her hand from her forehead to touch the young woman on the shoulder, I feel jealous.

Back at the farmhouse I offer to wash and steam the clams. Gillian goes upstairs to take a shower. When supper is ready, I carry the wicker table and two chairs from the porch to a shady spot on the lawn. To think I might have missed this—seeing the house and gardens, spending two days and a night with Gillian, sharing my loss, my fears, and my joys with her—if I hadn't listened to my heart.

Before I can call her to the table, Gillian steps off the porch, shining from her shower, in a pale shirt and slacks. She notices me blush in response, and says, "I see you found the wine."

We sit down at the table. Gillian smiles knowingly. She has seen through me, and I am both sorry and glad about that. I try to think of something to say other than what I'm thinking, but I'm struck dumb by self-consciousness. When Gillian asks me what's on my mind, I try to sound casual and sophisticated.

"Do you think bisexuality is a way of being for some, or a denial of the truth?"

"Are you asking me about your mom or you?" Gillian says, and again I feel the rush of blood to my cheeks.

"Do you think Mom was bisexual or just a late bloomer?" I ask.

"What do you think?" Gillian asks me.

"I believed her when she said she had once been in love with my dad."

"Me too," Gillian says. "I suspect there are as many ways of being as there are people. And it's for each to decide who she is."

"Could be I'm the late bloomer," I say.

"Or a reluctant heterosexual," Gillian says. "Many feminists are. Wasn't there a man in your life?"

"Yes. Once."

"Any women?" Gillian asks, after helping herself to a clam and indicating I did all right in the kitchen.

"A woman I photographed. We weren't intimate, but I thought about it. I never said anything to Mom about her, and I wish now that I had. The day Mom told me she was in love with you I was worrying I might be pregnant. I didn't tell her about that either."

"Have there been any others?" Gillian asks.

I hesitate before say, "There's you."

"What about me?" she asks.

"What about you?" I say, wondering how to tell her what I feel. "I was nervous about coming here," I say, "and it wasn't because you're strange."

Gillian puts down her fork and says, "Come on, let's go for a walk." We head out to the large oak tree beyond the gardens and chicken coop. Once there Gillian says, "I thought it might help us to move."

"Has it helped you?" I ask.

Gillian gives me a long look then steps close to me and kisses me gently on the mouth. When she steps back I instinctively reach for her.

"I think we better leave it at that," she says.

"Why?" I ask.

Gillian looks at me seriously, then says, "If you weren't Jean's daughter I'd want more than a kiss, and maybe because I was her lover, you do."

"Why the kiss then?" I ask.

"It seemed like the honest thing to do."

"You don't have to hold my parentage against me," I say. Gillian throws an arm around me, and we head back to the table.

"Some day when we're less vulnerable," she says.

"Would you like to see me again?" I ask, and she answers yes.

Back at the table we are different. Actually, Gillian is just as she was. The difference between us is me: I no longer feel like someone's daughter. Gillian, I realize, has regarded me independently all along. Why, then, did she say, *If I wasn't my mother's daughter?*

"Why do you think I'm attracted to you because of Mom?" I ask. "Why wouldn't that stop me?"

"It didn't," she says.

"And you feel it's because of her?"

"I think you identify with her."

"I don't think that's why," I say, "but it is complicated."

"Life is full of surprises," Gillian says beautifully. She hasn't killed our chance. She's postponed it.

Gillian pours some juice from her clams onto a saucer and puts the saucer on the grass beside her for her cat.

"What time is your friend coming tomorrow?" I ask.

"Early."

"I don't think I'll stick around to meet her."

"I didn't think you would."

"Do you ever get a few days off?" I ask.

"If you let me know in advance," Gillian says.

At my car, sometime later, I think of kissing Gillian good-bye. Before I can, she takes a strong hold of me and hugs me closely to her.

"Thank you for coming," she says.

Once I'm seated behind the wheel, Gillian leans in and kisses me. I don't want to leave.

She steps back from the car so I can turn it around. No, don't do this, I'm thinking, as I'm backing up, then heading down the drive.

Gillian walks briskly toward her house, not giving me an opening in which I can change my mind.

SIX

The rest of
that summer and fall I
work most days and every
night printing pictures of the family. I
have always preferred working at night when
the world is still. I don't seek any outside work and take
only the jobs that aren't time-consuming because I'm consumed by
my journey inward and backward. There is enough of Mom in me
to care only that I can afford the necessities. As long as I have the
resources to purchase film, chemicals, and paper, pay my rent and
eat, I'm content.

I begin selecting pictures I think are representative of us. But
after weeks of uninspired printing I start over, selecting photos that
touch me somehow, with no concern about how they will be seen
and judged by others. Thoughts of Gillian lead me to this. Her open-
ness is a reminder to me that confidence comes from listening to
an inner voice.

In my first darkroom session I had to do twenty prints of the
same photograph before I was happy with one. In the second go-
round often the first print is good, making the process seem too easy
at times.

Working from the heart, I stop searching for a purpose in the
work. I stop asking myself if I have the moral right to do what I'm

doing. I stop wondering if I'm fulfilling my mother's destiny with my interest in Gillian as I have assumed I was fulfilling Jeff's destiny by being a photographer. I stop trying to resolve my life and trust that the work will provide what I need.

What I learn on my journey inward and backward is simple: that I chose to be the undemanding child and denied myself some of what I needed and much of what I wanted. And that I must now hold myself responsible for those things.

During this period I behave in ways others would consider antisocial. I don't go out to movies or gallery openings. On the rare occasion when I run into someone I know I don't talk about myself or my work. And I don't call Gillian. I think about her daily, but I am not ready to venture further. My closest friend, Carol, becomes worried about my state of mind and plans a ski trip to Idaho over the Christmas holiday on my behalf.

By mid-December I think I've completed the work. All together there are sixty-four photos. Two-thirds of them are photos I've taken. Many of the others Jeff took. All are my prints. Some existing prints I re-photographed in the studio because I couldn't find their negatives. Then I experimented with toning, trying selenium, sepia, copper, and gold; deciding to use only selenium to make the photographs archival. The picture I select to be first in the book is of Dad and me ice-skating together. I am only six years old at the time. I choose this picture because I was afraid of the ice and only went out on it with Dad because he was a careful person. I knew if it was all right with him then it must be safe. Mom took this picture of us.

The second picture is of Mom straddling a boy's bicycle. She is twenty years old in the photo. Her pant legs are rolled up to her calves, and she has a wide open smile on her face. Dad took this picture of her. I think of her today as that young woman, raring to go.

The third picture in the book is a picture I took of Jeff flying out of the birch tree up at Lake Lydia. He is ten years old in the photo. He asked me to take the picture of him, and I'm glad I did.

It was months after Jeff's accident that I began photographing everything in sight with his camera. When the roll which was in the camera was developed there was a photo of Jeff on it, taken minutes before his accident. He is sitting in his new boat, poised like a big shot at the steering wheel with a grin on his face. I no longer see anything sad in this photo.

On that same roll of film was another of Jeff, taken by me many months later when Jeff first came home from the hospital. He is a thirteen-year-old boy wearing a white skull cap on his head. He has a soft mouth and round cheeks. He is lying on his side in bed. His eyes are open, but he is asleep behind them. At the time I expected Jeff to get better, to wake from his eyes-open unconsciousness once the wound on his head healed and the bandage was removed.

Also included in the book are two photos of Gillian: the first of her walking with Mom on the beach Christmas Day; and the second of her alone, in her garden, which I took when I visited Shelter Island.

Many of the photos chosen for the book do not show us at our best because I feel strongly that it is not just life's celebrations that affirm it.

Dad is carrying Jeff to the car in one of them, taking him to the hospital the year he got pneumonia. Jeff's face is expressionless. Dad's face shows grave concern. In another, Dad is sitting on a lawn chair, his eyes half closed, holding a drink.

There is a photo of Mom hoeing her garden with a frown on her face, and another of her sitting on the porch, reading a book, unaware of Dad next to her, crying. I took that picture without either of them being aware of me or the camera.

Dad took the picture of me standing in my high school graduation gown at Jeff's bedside, posing unhappily for him. He took another of me I wished he hadn't at the time. I'm pouting over learning I haven't been accepted at the Rochester Institute of Technology.

And there is the Christmas photo Dad insisted I take of Mom and him on the couch, huddled next to Jeff; the photo of Mom, half naked, revealing her mastectomy scar; and a photo of me taken late one night during the process of putting the book together. I had my tripod up, photographing old prints, when I got the urge to turn the camera and the lights on me. It is a picture of a haggard face. It doesn't show the joy or surprise I often feel doing my work. It does show my doggedness.

Together the portraits reveal four lives lived together happily and sadly, heroically and cowardly.

It is early December when I get the call from Carol saying she and John are organizing a ski vacation to Sun Valley. Carol is surprised that I need no encouragement to agree to join them and five others.

Over the months I had written to Dad but he hadn't answered any of my letters. I didn't deceive him about what I was doing, and he didn't support me in it. I wasn't invited to spend Christmas with him and didn't assume I was welcome. I go with my friends to Idaho.

Three days after Christmas I am playing Scrabble when I get a call from Meg Benson. She has been trying to reach me since Dad had a stroke on Christmas Day.

Meg called my apartment in the City, as well as family friends, but no one knew where I was. It wasn't until Bob was going through Dad's Christmas cards and found mine that they discovered I was in Sun Valley.

Dad had a second stroke at the hospital and died early on the morning of December 26th.

I leave Idaho the next morning. When I arrive at LaGuardia

I take a taxi into the City to get appropriate clothes. I will stay overnight at my apartment and drive to Old Field the following day.

seven

Two morn-
ings later I wake in Old
Field. The sheets at the bot-
tom of the bed are cold. I pull my legs
back up where it's warm and recall the night
before: Dad's memorial service, Ted and Chris following
me home, washing and changing Jeff when the Rooneys left, the
quiet in the house, and wishing I weren't so alone.

I didn't expect to be without parents before I was one myself. . . I
wonder if anyone has the life they expect. I feel badly that my last
conversation with Dad was an argument, that I left the house that
day, as I so often did, challenging him. Why did I challenge Dad?
What did I hope to win or convince him of? Why was I so angry?

I wanted to be inspired by my father and I wasn't. I wanted Dad
to be my hero. But Dad was tied up, unable to inspire himself let
alone others.

I loved my Dad, and I knew he loved me. Why wasn't that
enough? If he were here now I wouldn't feel so alone. When I had
his companionship I took it for granted and demanded more. I'm
sorry, Dad. I'm sorry I wasn't more grateful.

I get out of bed and call John Mueller from the hall phone on
the second floor. I'm not yet dressed. I have on my pajamas and
Mom's cardigan sweater. I spoke to John briefly at the funeral home

but didn't explain to him why I would be calling this morning.

The nurse puts me on hold, and while I wait I gaze out the window overlooking the roof of the porch at the back of the house. Jeff and I once climbed out that window, crawled over to the blue spruce which towers over the porch, clambered into its thick body and down its trunk to the ground below. I don't remember the reason. I do remember being itchy afterward and not telling Mom why my arms had broken out in hives.

John asks me if I slept all right.

"Good enough," I say, then explain to him why I'm calling.

He doesn't seem surprised. He advises me to set up a humidifier to keep Jeff's eyes and nasal passages moist and says he will stop by the house on his way home that night. After hanging up the phone, I go downstairs to see Jeff. He is asleep. I sit beside the bed and look at him. His hair is long and lank, and he needs a shave. I touch his hand. It is warm but unresponsive. I feel sorry that Mom has not been able to take care of him these last years, and I wish for his sake that it were she, not me, who would be letting him go. It ought to be her, I think. She would know just how to do it. She would make it noble. She had never rejected him as I have. It ought to be someone who isn't suspect.

I look at the cans of Sustacal stacked on the table near the bed. What do I do with them, I wonder, and I start to cry. It is an angry cry. I'm mad at Mom and Dad and God for leaving this up to me. Why me? They should have done this years ago so I wouldn't have to. I drop my head and shoulders and weep. What a fraud I am. I rejected this Jeff because he looked peculiar and smelled bad. I accused Mom and Dad of deluding themselves, but it wasn't strength of character which lead me to say with certainty that Jeff no longer lived in this body. I didn't like this Jeff so I pretended to know with certainty that this was not Jeff, that this was only skin and bones.

If I believed Jeff were not here then why was it so important to me that he be released? If I didn't believe his soul was somehow or other committed to his body as long as it lived, then I wouldn't feel the nurturing of his body was holding him back. Why did I let the smell get in my way? What kind of person would let so small a thing get in her way?

Oh, god, I don't want Jeff to feel I reject him. I don't want him to feel any pain. I want him to be happy. That's all I want, just for Jeff to be happy.

With that thought a remarkable thing happens. It is as though a window in the room opens and a breeze blows in. And on the breeze words of reassurance are spoken. The muscles in my body relax, my mind lets go. I get up from the chair and slowly pull the feeding tube from Jeff's nose. It feels as though someone is helping me, as it sometimes feels in the darkroom. "Thank you, thank you, thank you," I say to whoever is there.

I will fast with Jeff that first day. Eventually, I go upstairs and dress, then return downstairs to cut Jeff's hair and wash and shave him. I take my time washing Jeff's body. I have nothing else in the world to do. This is all that is important, and I do it slowly. When I'm done, I don't make up a fresh bed for Jeff. I lift him up into a sitting position, pull him over onto my shoulder, and lift him off the bed. He is not as light as he appears, but I am stronger than I thought. I start for the stairs. God help me, I think, as I start up them. I don't want to drop Jeff.

At the top of the stairs we are flooded in sunlight coming from the hall window. I step from that sunlight into Jeff's dark room and lower him onto his bed, then go to the windows and open the curtains to let in as much sunlight as possible. When I look back at Jeff, lying on his bed, I'm disheartened. He looks strange here. Did I expect a thirteen-year-old boy? Why did I move him? Who did I do that for? I feel a frightful sadness crawl up my insides from my stomach to my throat. I'm sorry, Jeff. Should I take you down where you belong, or leave you be now that you are here? Which would be better? I don't know what is right.

Maybe if he were in the bed, not lying on top of it, he would look more at home. I roll Jeff over onto his side, lift the covers and roll Jeff onto the bottom sheet, straighten him out, and cover him. The summer blanket and light spread are not enough. Jeff's body is starting to feel cool.

I walk across the hall to the guest room, but the door is locked. I'd forgotten about that. I go to my room, take the wool blanket off my bed, and return to Jeff. He will be all right now, I think. I'm getting used to him here. But the room is dirty.

I go get the vacuum and a bucket of sudsy water.

It is dark by the time I finish cleaning Jeff's room. It smells clean. I have my confidence back. I'm doing O.K. now.

I've just finished my shower when the doorbell rings. I pull my pajama top down over my head, grab Mom's sweater, and hurry downstairs. It is John Mueller.

He doesn't ask me why I've moved Jeff upstairs. After examining Jeff and listening to his heart and lungs, John and I go back downstairs.

I offer John something to drink, and we go to the kitchen. We sit at the table while John has a glass of orange juice. He tells me that Jeff appears healthy.

"This may take a while," he says. "It could be weeks."

I listen and say nothing.

"Don't you think you should get someone to help you, to be with you? A family member or a friend? Is there anyone?" John asks.

"Not really," I say. "No family. Only cousins I don't know, who don't live here."

"What about a good friend?"

"I don't think so," I say. "I don't know how they would feel about this. And I wouldn't want to have to explain everything."

"Isn't there someone who feels as you do? Someone you wouldn't have to explain yourself to?"

"No," I say, although I think of Gillian.

"I'll come by, of course."

"You don't have to do that," I say.

"I will."

"I'll call you if I need you," I say.

"Don't you think some company would be good?"

"I do all right on my own," I say.

"I know you do, you're a remarkable woman. I didn't mean to imply—"

"You didn't," I say, thinking I'm anything but remarkable.

When John leaves I turn off the lights downstairs and return upstairs. I sit with Jeff and read "Where I Lived, And What I Lived For" from *Walden*. My eyelids are heavy by the time I reach, *Time is but the stream I go a-fishing in.*

I finish reading the last paragraph in the chapter: . . . *I have always been regretting that I was not as wise as the day I was born. The intellect is a cleaver; it discerns and rifts its way into the secret of things. I do not wish to be any more busy with my hands than is necessary.*

I lie down beside Jeff, under the covers, and fall asleep.

It isn't yet dawn when I wake and go to my room to use the bathroom. As I start to get into my bed I realize it has no blanket, and I remember again that the guest room is locked. I could get the key now, or the blanket off Dad's bed, or go back to Jeff. I decide to go down to the kitchen and look in the junk drawer for the master key. It is there.

I'm hungry, so I pour myself a glass of orange juice before head-

ing back upstairs. Is Jeff hungry, I wonder. John said, no, he would
not be. Jeff would be unaware of his body's hunger just as he is unaware of his surroundings. But is he? Is he entirely unaware? How
does John know for certain? When I return upstairs I look in on
Jeff. He's asleep.

I don't know what to expect in the guest room, what Dad con-
sidered out-of-bounds, and I'm curious but cautious. I open the door
only slightly and look in.

The room appears as though someone were living in it, as
though Mom were living here. Her robe is draped across the bed,
and her slippers are on the floor beside it. A sweater hangs from
the back of Mom's reading chair, an open book is resting on the
ottoman, and there is darning yarn and a pair of sewing scissors on
the table beside the chair. In the basket on the floor are socks to
be mended, Dad's socks. Mom's comb and brush and mirror are
on the dresser. Her watch is laid out as though she had just taken
it off. The closet in the room is full of Mom's clothes, including her
wedding dress. The drawers in the dresser are full of her things—
underwear, scarves, gloves, belts, and a purse I never saw Mom carry.
The room even smells like Mom, like the cologne she used to wear.
What is this? None of this stuff was here after Mom died. All of it
has been placed here, purposefully, gathered from other rooms in
the house and brought here for display. I know what this is, and
it scares me to realize how like him I am. Didn't I just yesterday carry
Jeff upstairs to his room, the room I insisted be kept just as it was
the day of his accident, the room I needed to hold onto when Jeff
slipped away from me?

I step over to the ottoman and pick up the book. It is a book
on the Pine Barrens. Mom was so inspired by the book she made
a trip to the New Jersey wilderness to see it for herself. She must
have wished she could take Jeff with her. She and Jeff had shared

a love of nature and had gone off together on many hikes when Jeff was able.

I take the blanket off Mom's bed, the book, and Mom's watch from the dresser, and unlock the door to our joint bathroom. I put the watch on my wrist, get into my bed with the book, and fall asleep.

When I wake it is late morning. The phone in the hall is ringing. It is Meg Benson apologizing for missing Dad's memorial service. I ask her how she is feeling, and she says she would like to see me. When I hesitate, she says, "If you have company I can come later or tomorrow."

"Who would I have?" I say, surprised by her conclusion.

"I don't know," she says. "A friend?"

"No. I'm alone. It's just I'm not dressed yet."

"Don't bother," Meg says, but I do.

The phone rings three times while I'm getting dressed. The first caller is John Mueller, the second, a client of Dad's, and the third, Dad's lawyer. I pull the phone out of the hall jack and take it to Jeff's room to plug in.

While I wait for Meg to arrive, I change Jeff's diaper. As I'm doing that I see Jeff, in my mind's eye, in his Davy Crockett hat. Jeff was told to hang the hat in the mud room when he came in because it smelled to high heaven. But even without the hat Jeff sometimes smelled like wet fur.

I take the dirty diaper to the bathroom. On my way back I remember something else: Jeff sitting on the Calhoun's garage roof.

Tom and Mary Calhoun were neighborhood friends. Tom was my age, Mary a year younger. A fifth child, Brian Skinner, who was in Jeff's class, also played with us. It was a summer's eve, and the five of us were playing hide-and-seek. Jeff climbed up the lattice on the side of the Calhoun's garage and hid on the roof. He was only seven years old at the time and very serious about games. He was still waiting to be found when it grew dark and I went home to tell Dad I didn't know where Jeff was.

Dad and I scoured the neighborhood looking for him. When Jeff finally saw Dad, he called down, "Hey, you looking for me?"

"Holy Toledo!" Dad hollered. "What are you doing up there?"

"Come see," Jeff said.

"No, you get down here. We've been worried about you."

"How come you're worried about me?" Jeff asked.

"Because it's dark out."

"I watched it from up here, and it was beautiful, Dad."

"How did you get up there?"

"I climbed the ladder."

"What ladder?"

"The one on the side."

"That's not a ladder."

"Bern says it is."

"It's lattice, Jeff. *Lattice*, not *ladder*." Dad gave me a look that asked whether I put Jeff up to this. Then he reached up and grabbed a hold of Jeff's legs which were dangling over the edge of the roof, searching for something to step onto.

"Christ Almighty, you kids," Dad said, but he didn't sound mad. I think he was impressed.

The doorbell rings, and I'm startled out of my reverie.

Moments later, Meg embraces me and says, "I told you not to bother getting dressed. I almost came over in my robe. How are you doing, Bern?"

I say I'm O.K. and offer Meg some coffee. She follows me to the kitchen and when she passes the dining room she looks in. "You really are alone," she says. "Where's Jeff?"

"He's upstairs," I answer, and don't explain.

Meg takes a seat at the kitchen table, and I join her a few minutes later with coffee for both of us.

"Rumor has it you're going to sell the house," she says.

"Are you concerned?"

"No. I thought maybe you could use some help packing."

"I'm not in any hurry," I say. "I won't put it on the market until spring."

"I'd like to help you when you do."

"Thanks. I'm going to speak to Dad's lawyer about giving Mom's half of the garden to you. I don't know what that will entail, but whatever, I want you to have it."

"Bern, that's not why I'm here."

"I know."

"Have you decided what you will do about Jeff?"

"Yes." I look at Meg wondering if I should tell her. She holds my gaze and waits. "I'm going to let him go," I say. "Not to a nursing home. I think he'd rather be with Mom and Dad."

"I think so, too," Meg says.

"I'm sitting with him until that happens."

Meg nods her head and asks, "Is it difficult?"

"I'm pretty mixed up about it. I'm not sure what I believe or feel sometimes."

"My mother used to tell me it was a good sign when I was confused because it meant my mind wasn't set, and a mind that isn't set is open."

"Thanks, Meg."

"Beware of folks who are never confused."

I return her smile. "Are you hungry?" I ask. "I need to eat something. I could fix us some eggs or a sandwich."

"Fix yourself something," she says. "And pour me another cup of coffee."

With my back to Meg, frying an egg on the stove, I ask Meg if she ever met Gillian. She says she did, and I ask her what she thought.

"She's an attractive woman."

"Did you like her?" I ask.

"That's what I meant."

"Oh, I thought you meant she was attractive-looking."

"She is that," Meg answers. "Have you been in touch with her?"

"I saw her last summer for the first time since Mom died."

"How was it?"

I take my plate over to the table and sit. "It was wonderful. And confusing," I add.

Meg waits, knowing there's more.

"I'm attracted to her."

"That's nice," she says.

"I mean *attracted* to her."

"I understand. That's nice."

"Do you really think so?"

"Sure. Why not?"

"For starters because I'm a woman."

"Women have been loving women for ages. I don't know why people act so surprised by it, or object. What's to object to, really?"

"Some people think it's unnatural."

"People who haven't spent any time in nature," Meg says, making me smile.

"Did you and Mom talk about this?" I ask.

"Sure, we talked about everything."

"You must miss that."

"I do. I haven't got a good friend like her. Except Bob. And that isn't exactly the same."

"I was glad to see him yesterday," I say.

"He wants me to ask you if you would like him to look over your Dad's papers—pay bills that are due and get his taxes ready."

"I haven't even thought of that," I say. "Yes, I could use his help."

"You can get them together and give them to me, or Bob could work on them here. Whichever is the easiest for you."

"Everything should be up in Dad's studio. If Bob wants to come over, that would be great, but I could have Dad's lawyer and tax man handle that."

"Let Bob. He can get in touch with the right people. And I'll help you pack when the time comes."

"I don't know when that will be," I say.

"I understand. I'm available whenever."

"Have you and Bob seen Anna recently?" I ask.

"Yes. We had her here for Christmas."

"How is she doing?"

"When she's on her medication she does pretty well."

"How old is Anna now?"

"She'll be thirty-two this year."

"Jeff would be twenty-seven," I say, and Meg asks me if she can see Jeff.

On our way upstairs I tell Meg about the time Jeff and I set the basement on fire. "It was a cold, rainy day and we were playing scouts in the basement. We built a fire in our tee-pee, a blanket thrown over a card table, with wood shavings we found under Dad's wood-working table. Naturally, the blanket caught on fire, and Mom had to come to our rescue, dousing the fire with buckets of water from the laundry tub. And the laundry which was hanging up in the base-ment nearly caught on fire, too. It had to be washed again because of the smoke smell. I remember how tired Mom looked afterward, and feeling guilty for making her so tired. . . ."

Meg touches my arm as we step into Jeff's room.

"I've been remembering a lot of things today," I say. When Meg lets go of me, she steps over to Jeff and sits down on the edge of his bed.

After a while she says to Jeff, "When you see your mom, you tell her I miss her." Meg brushes Jeff's hair off his forehead as she did to me the day Mom died, and says, "You'll be O.K., Jeff. Bern will be with you until your mom comes to get you."

Then she looks up at me with tears in her eyes. "It's the right thing to do, Bern. I feel it, too."

When Meg gets up I put my arms around her. "You'll be all right, Bern. Don't be afraid of not understanding everything. We can't."

"Do you think Jeff is suffering?" I ask her.

"No, I don't think so. But if he does it won't last. He'll get through it with your help."

"The doctor says it will probably take a couple of weeks because Jeff's in good health."

"Bern, wouldn't you like someone to sit with you?"

"I don't think so," I say.

"To spell you for an hour?"

I shake my head. "I want to be with him when he dies."

"I want you to call me every day. Do you hear me?"

"I will."

I say good-bye to Meg at the door, then go to the dining room to get the tape recorder to take upstairs.

In Jeff's room I call the hospital supply people who rent us the hospital bed and tell them they can pick up the bed and other paraphernalia. I will also give them the surplus cans of Sustacal and the diapers Jeff won't need.

Hours later, when they have come and gone and the dining room is bare of everything but the bedside table and a couple of chairs, I hurry upstairs to Jeff, needing to reassure myself that I still have him. It is a moment of clarity for me, realizing that I do consider Jeff a part of life. It will be harder than I imagined to let go of him.

I put music on that I hope will keep me from crying and sit down at Jeff's desk, planning to write notes. Instead I open Jeff's desk drawer and examine its contents, touching and smelling everything: the pencils, the ruler, the rubber bands, Jeff's baseball cards, and coins, and chewing gum, the Indian head, the red dice, the lens cap, and the tiny nickel goat that once belonged to a farm set we played with. I will be able to let go of the furnishings of the house, but not these things, and not Dad's wallet which I find in the top drawer of his dresser, and not Mom's thimbles which I take from the sewing basket in the sewing room, and not the photographs throughout the house. After dinner that night I go from room to room, taking photos out of their frames.

When I return to Jeff, lying still in his bed, I think about the photographer he would have been—a fine art photographer of nature, not a photojournalist like me. The marsh, the beach, the roads he walked, and the trees he climbed were what he preferred to photograph.

I haven't included many of Jeff's best photos in my book of family photos because they're of the land. Why haven't I realized their importance until now, that it's not only the people we relate to but the places we choose that show who we are?

The next morning Carol calls me from the City to ask if anything is wrong. I've been away longer than she expected I would be. I tell her why I'm still in Old Field, and she asks me if I'm sure I want to do this alone. I say I'm sure and wonder why everyone thinks I would be better off with company. The best part of my days and nights are when I'm alone with Jeff, listening to music or reading to him. Every interruption is an intrusion. And the painful moments are the most precious because it's the pain which lets me know how much I love him.

That day I spend several hours washing Jeff and rubbing lotion into his skin. His body has always troubled me because it's abnormal looking. But the longer I am with it, and the closer I look at it, the less strange it seems. I begin to see it as Jeff would, as Jeff saw the inhabitants of a marsh. Maybe I would no longer think the marsh was yucky.

That evening, Bob Benson and Meg arrive. Meg has dinner with her. Bob will look over Dad's papers after we eat while Meg sits with Jeff and I go for a drive. Meg insists I leave the house for at least an hour.

"Do anything," she says. "Go to a movie or sit on a park bench, but go out."

"Why?" I ask her.

"Because I want some time alone with your brother," she says.

I can't argue with that. I drive out to Greenport, where the ferry crosses over to Shelter Island, and stand on the pier for close to an hour. Why is it I always run here? What is it that draws me to her no matter how much time passes?

At home the dishes are done, coffee is brewed, and Bob is wiping the counter tops. It is late not to have gotten started on Dad's papers. I suggest that Bob do it another night or on the weekend, and he tells me he's got it all in a box to take home with him.

I'm glad Bob won't be coming back to work in the studio. Not that I didn't enjoy his and Meg's company, but I want the freedom privacy allows me. I would be self-conscious reading aloud to Jeff if someone else were in the house, or singing to Elton John, or getting in bed with Jeff. Since Jeff's first night upstairs I have crawled into bed with him each night to read to him. I did it the first night because I was cold. I do it now because I've overcome the unpleasant-ness of his body. For fourteen years I was ashamed of my revulsion. Now I feel better about myself as well. I open a favorite book and read: *They were summers of the senses. Softened, muted, gentle senses that gave beauty to the eye, music to the ear, and the silken feel of sand and water to the touch. They were pockets of memory, sealed and com-plete in themselves, creating a lasting impression in the mind and heart of a child.*

Jeff remains asleep all day the following day. When I speak to John Mueller he says that Jeff will probably stay asleep now.

"How will he die?" I ask.

John says, "He's becoming weak. When his heart and lungs are too weak to keep him alive, he will die."

"Will that hurt?"

"He's unaware of what's happening, Bern."

"Sometimes I feel he is aware."

"You feel his presence?"

"Yes."

"But he's not connected to his body as you and I are. He can-not feel his body."

That night I sense sadness in Jeff, and I ask him if he hurts. I feel something more than my sadness. It is like the time Mom told Jeff he had to give the puppy back, and Jeff and I cried together.

Jeff's Pentax became his pet. He took it everywhere with him. Maybe I did the same. Maybe I didn't take it to fulfill his destiny. Maybe I took it because I, too, wanted something to love with me at all times.

I set up my tripod and take a picture of Jeff and me in bed to-gether.

The next day I write to Gillian. I tell her Dad has died and I am sitting with Jeff until he does. I tell her I worked all summer and fall on the family pictures and thought I was finished, but then Dad died and I came home and discovered I had more pictures to take. I tell Gillian I drove out to Greenport one night and stood on the pier. I don't apologize for not writing or calling sooner, nor explain why I haven't. I ask her if she remembers Mom's Bulova watch, and I tell her I am sending it to her because I think Mom would want her to have it. I say I will be packing up the house one of these days and will probably be sending her other things which she may or may not want.

Days later, Gillian writes back, saying she is sorry my father has died and since my letter she has thought of little else but me and Jeff. She says I'm welcome to come see her anytime, and that she is pleased to have Mom's watch. She says she is anxious to see the photos and then adds, *I have missed you.*

Jeff dies that day. I am sitting at his desk with my back to him, writing to Carol in the City, and something causes me to turn and look at Jeff. The quiet, perhaps.

I remember, as a young girl, coloring a picture of Jesus in Sunday school. He was sitting on a rock with children all around him.

I touch Jeff's face and bent arm. He was always a child. And I, always a child with him. We were children together, and how happy we were.

eight

two months later

The first
warm day in March I
drive up to Lake Lydia. I have-
n't been there in years, and never alone, and
I'm concerned about how it will look, how I will get along
on my own there. The narrow road into the cabin has become over-
grown with tall grass and weeds, and I nearly miss the turn-off onto
it. The same wild and rampant growth has sprouted up around the
cabin, and a large limb from a nearby pine appears to have broken
from its trunk in a storm and landed on the roof.

Walking up the sandy path to the door, I notice that a window
shutter has come off two of its hinges to hang cockeyed. I pause at
the door, afraid of what I'll find inside. But aside from ashes blown
into the room from the fireplace, a layer of dust on everything, and
cobwebs strung across the windows, it looks as I remember it. To
my relief, the tree limb did not break through the roof.

I open the shutters and windows, take everything I can lift out
to the dock, and shake out the blankets, then return to the cabin
to shovel ashes from the fireplace, dust, and sweep, and wash the
walls, floors, and windows.

Without stopping to rest, I climb up onto the roof, throw the
tree limb off, and pull leaves out of the rain gutters. It is exhausting

work, and I don't know what's gotten into me, unless Mom's spirit has possessed me.

As the sun starts to set, I climb down from the roof, strip down to nothing, and take a towel and a bar of soap out to the dock. The water is frigid. I am out of it almost as quickly as I got in. The hell with soaping up.

I didn't stop on the way to get groceries. Since there is nothing in the cabin to eat, I go to bed hungry and wake, famished, in the morning.

Along the road to town I pass the one gas station and Woody's. The last time I was in either place I was with Mom. This is how it will be for a while, I tell myself.

I sit on the grocer's porch, beside the Coke machine, and eat an orange and a sugar doughnut. I wonder how difficult it would be to have plumbing and electricity put in the cabin.

It's not quite ten o'clock when I get back. Only a pair of coots are out on the lake. I sit on the dock and watch them, eating two more doughnuts. I didn't realize I had so much sadness in me. My chest heaves, and I start to cry. Maybe if I had someone I wouldn't miss Mom so much. At this stage in my life I should be a mom, not be wanting one I tell myself, but that doesn't stop me from crying.

When the coots fly off I get up and go repair the shutter. When that is done I right the boat, hope it hasn't any serious leaks, and drag it down to the dock to lower it into the water.

I am out on the lake a good hour when I begin to feel lonely again. I row back. The physical exertion of rowing, or doing any-thing, helps keep my mind off what is missing in my life.

I take a walk in the woods, to collect pine cones and firewood. I will definitely buy a woodburning stove. The fireplace isn't efficient for warming the cabin. And I'll look into plumbing and electricity. It would be nice to have a refrigerator and toilet. But I will keep the kerosene lamps.

I dump my load of firewood at the back door and gaze out across the lake at the mountains Mom loved.

nine

a month later

It has been al-
most a year. She is
dressed in pants and a jacket,
not shorts, and her suntan has faded.
She walks briskly, full of confidence, toward
me. I'm on the dock, waiting. She doesn't call out my
name or wave, but she is smiling, and so am I. When she reaches
me we embrace and kiss, a friendly kiss, and look at one another.

"I didn't think it would be so long," she says. "If I'd known it
would be, I don't think I would have let you go."

"I'm sorry," I say. "I wanted to see you—to be with you. But I
had some things to do before I saw you again. I didn't want to come
to you needing a mother. And I honestly didn't understand my feel-
ings and didn't want to hurt yours."

"I appreciate that."

"I'm still not all that sure about myself. I can imagine what
others will think of me with my mother's lover. I may be confused
at times."

"Bern, be quiet and let me look at you." Gillian puts her hand
on my mouth, then touches my hair. "When you left I kicked myself. I had a chance to be loved by someone passionate and dear,
and I let you go. When you didn't call I told myself that's good, good

for her. I'm too old for her. I've got a history. Whoever she ends up with will make her happier than I can."

"Excuse me, may I speak now?"

"Yes, as long as you don't say I'm too old for you or you're too closely related to my last lover."

"I'd like to strip down and go swimming with you, then build a fire and lay next to you."

Gillian gives me a long look, then smiles and bends down to test the water. "Even Jean wouldn't swim in water this cold," she says, but, having said that, Gillian takes off her shoes and socks and un-buttons the waist of her pants.

"That's all right," I say, stopping her from undressing any fur-ther. "Let's go to the cabin."

A fire is already burning in the fireplace. Gillian removes her jacket and stands with her backside to it. I am only feet away from her when she begins to unbutton her blouse. We look at one an-other and are silent. I am startled and pleased by what she is do-ing. When Gillian's blouse is loose, hanging from her shoulders, she invites me to her and places my hands on her hips, inviting me to touch her. Her skin is warm and smooth. Her breasts are full. I can feel her eyes on me as I take her in. When I lift mine, we kiss and then I pull away and remove my sweater and the T-shirt beneath it. We are nearly the same height. I feel Gillian's warm flesh against mine, then her hands on my back. We kiss again, and when we pull away this time, we remove the rest of our clothes and stand before one another naked.

"I wanted to find you passionate," she says, "but I was afraid to hope for it."

We embrace, and I can feel Gillian's legs against mine as well as her breasts. It is at once a comfort and exciting. Gillian runs her hands along my sides to my thighs, then boldly, she slides a hand between my legs.

I won't be able to stand, I think, and I pull away from her to get a blanket off the nearest bunk. We sit together in front of the fire, Gillian behind me, her legs straddling mine and her breasts against my back. She kisses my neck and begins to stroke me. I want to see her while she does this. Not being able to is a tease. Finally, Gillian allows me to turn around and face her as she makes love to me. It is her face, full of feeling, that I have fallen in love with.

My head is resting in the hollow above her breasts when I orgasm. She hums softly, echoing my happiness. I could never have imagined how good it feels to be loved by a woman, to feel a woman's lips, hands, breasts, and full body on mine. Perhaps it is not because she is a woman but because she is Gillian. That I don't know.

I lower my body onto Gillian's and place my tongue between her legs. I know what feels good to me, what excites me. As Gillian stirs under me, I feel powerful. When her back arches, she holds my shoulders with her two hands and cries out. I kiss her breasts, neck, and mouth, then run my hands through her hair, pulling it away from her face, looking into her eyes and at her mouth which is smiling slightly. "I love you," I say.

It is too cold to lie only on top of a blanket. I get a second one off the other bunk to cover us. Because I feel unconstrained and natural in Gillian's arms, I can admit that I was once scared of her.

"Or to be completely honest, scared of how I felt about you," I say. "But it was the kind of scare that made me hungry."

Gillian kisses my neck, whispers she loves me, then slides down to kiss my breasts with an open mouth and runs her tongue across my belly to my legs. As I rise and fall she holds onto me tightly.

We sleep together for a couple of hours before Gillian gets up and leaves me alone in front of the fire. When I wake I'm afraid she is gone. But then I see her nestled on one of the bunks. I don't disturb her. I crawl up to the loft to sleep there the rest of the night.

In the morning when I come down I see Gillian huddled under a blanket out on the dock. It is a brisk day, but the sky is clear and the sun it out. Gillian turns when she hears me. I see she is crying. Is this when she tells me she misses my mother, that I'm not Jean? Instead she says, "I didn't think this would happen to me again."

"You're happy?" I ask, and she nods her head. "Then why are you crying?"

Gillian doesn't answer, and I worm my way under her blanket. "Do you often cry when you're happy?" I ask.

"I cry when I'm deeply touched," she says, and she puts her arm around me and draws me to her.

I look across the lake at Mom's mountains and wonder at all of life.

Before making plans for the day—to dress and take the trail through the woods to town for breakfast—I ask Gillian to tell me something she has never told a soul. She looks at me silently for several minutes, and I wonder, is there nothing about her she hasn't told someone? Then in a quiet voice, Gillian says, "I overheard my mother tell my grandmother that she didn't want to take me to Texas. She wanted to go down there with Drake and start a new life and a new family. So I went to my grandmother and told her I didn't want to go to Texas, I wanted to stay with her."

"My god, Gillian, how old were you?"

"Six."

"Shit."

"It was a good thing as it turned out. I loved my grandmother almost as much as life itself."

"But to hear your mother say she didn't want you."

"You know, Bern, I wasn't surprised. We rarely are. We know how people feel about us before they speak the words."

"Did you know I loved you?"

"I had an idea you found me interesting."

"All right," I say. "I'll tell you something I've never told anyone. The morning Mom came to my bedroom to invite me down to breakfast with you and her, informing me that you had stayed the night, I was jealous. But I wasn't jealous of you for having Mom's attention. I was jealous of her because she had you. It was too confusing and, I suppose, frightening for me to face. Being attracted to a woman is one thing, but your mother's lover? Jesus, I felt shoddy—a liar, a traitor, and perhaps even a queer. Yes, I find you interesting, like a bolt of lightning."

Gillian laughs and musses my hair. It is something a mother might do to her naughty daughter, and I am sensitive to that and slightly hurt. I don't want to be taken lightly.

ten

I put the
house in Old Field on the
market, the cabin on hold, and spend
the weekends that summer on Shelter Island.

Gillian has full days every Saturday and Sunday, and time
for me comes after sunset and before sunrise. In June and July I go
back to bed after having breakfast with Gillian, get up late, and set
out on photo excursions around the island.

After weeks of photographing landscapes I return to my prefer-
ence for people, shooting the bent bodies, sweaty brows, and cal-
lused hands of the women and men at work in the gardens and
greenhouse. My favorite camera that summer is a plastic Diana camera with an imperfect lens that gives dreamlike pictures. My favorite subject is Gillian.

It takes me several days to adjust to the City each time I return
to it. It isn't until Wednesday that I begin to enjoy my privacy. Oddly
enough, although I am never without a sense of longing for Gillian, on Friday it is sometimes hard to pull myself away from my
work, especially if I'm working in the darkroom.

Only once during the summer does Gillian come into the City
to surprise me. She is sitting on the steps of the brownstone when
I return from a day of shooting on Ellis Island. It is after 8:00 P.M.
Her face and form are glowing with the orange light of a setting sun.

I am weary, and she is a sight for sore eyes.

I call out when I see her. She rises.

"What's wrong?" I ask because she isn't smiling.

"I missed you."

"Come in," I say.

I haven't anything to offer Gillian; my refrigerator is bare. I eat out every night that I don't fix myself a bowl of soup or cereal.

"Take a long shower," I say, setting down my camera bag. "and I'll get us some Chinese."

When I return to the apartment Gillian is out of the shower, wrapped in my terry cloth robe. We sit together on the couch and eat out of the cartons.

"I was listening to some music today," she says. "It reminded me of Jean."

I don't know what to say. I thought missing me was the source of her sadness, not Mom. "I'm sorry," I answer.

"I haven't played that particular tape since—in a long time."

"It seems like yesterday," I say, now sadly aware of my own loss.

"I'm sorry, Bern. I come to you because you're the one who understands, but—"

"It's O.K.," I interrupt.

Gillian puts down her carton and chopsticks and asks, "Will you make love to me?"

Gillian shudders and begins to cry when I touch her. I hold her in my arms and wonder if this is how she was when Mom died. I wish that I had been with her then. I could easily make love to her, but instead I get down a favorite book from my shelf. I am reminded of how consoling my mother's voice was, how protected I felt when she crawled into my bed to read to me. I want to be all she was.

Gillian leans her head against me and closes her eyes as I read an Elizabeth Bishop poem. When she begins to breath deeply and

I am certain she is asleep, I cover her with a light blanket and go to bed.

In the morning I ask Gillian what music she had played.

She tells me, "It's a tape of Mary Black singing Irish folk songs."

"When did you and Mom listen to it?"

"We danced to it," she answers.

"Don't tell me any more," I say, then, after a moment, "We've never danced."

"Would you like to?" she asks.

Gillian knows me well enough now to read my face. I'm afraid of being less of a dancer than my mother. She takes me into her arms and makes love to me instead.

On July 4th, Judy and Phyllis from Orient, Peg from the City, and Janice from Greenport arrive on Shelter Island. Phyllis has been with Judy the last twenty-five years. Before that Judy and Gillian were lovers. Janice is a friend of Peg's; they are not lovers. Both appear interested in Gillian and aren't shy about showing their interest in my presence. The five have a long history and spend hours recalling it to one another. I am irked by the lot, Gillian also because she makes no attempt to bring me into the conversation. My mother's name comes up more than once or twice: *Remember when Jean said thus and such? Oh, Jean was great. It was Jean who did that. No one but Jean could.*

When I complain to Gillian that her friends ignored me, she asks me why I didn't complain to them.

"I was hoping you would say something," I answer.

"Speak up for Jean's little girl?"

"Then you heard Peg call me that."

"Yes."

"How did it make you feel?"

"Lucky. She's jealous. You might have noticed that."

"I noticed you were having a wonderful time without me."

"If you felt excluded you should have said something."

"Like, *Excuse me, but would you all go to hell?*"

"That would get their attention," Gillian says, smiling.

"And upset you."

"You take care of you, and I'll take care of me."

"You must have liked that about Mom," I say, at once hurt by Gillian and Mom for being hard on me.

"Bern, your mother was not the only one in my life. If you want to compare yourself to a half dozen I'll provide you with the names and personalities."

"Why are you being this way?" I ask.

"Treating you as a peer?"

By Labor Day I am more confident of my relationship with Gillian and looking forward to standing up for myself. Despite my protestations, I am drawn to Gillian because she expects that of me.

We are putting up an umbrella to shade us when Peg says, "I wish Jean were here to do this."

I ask Peg if she is trying to make me feel like a poor substitute, and for a moment all conversation stops. Judy laughs out of embarrassment and Phyllis asks, "Are you, Peg?"

Peg turns and walks into the house.

"She had a crush on Jean," Janice explains.

"She did?" asks Gillian.

"What about the rest of you?" I say. "Does everyone wish I were my mother?"

Gillian shakes her head as Phyllis calls out to Peg, "You can come back, she's mad at us all."

With that, I snap open the heavy umbrella on my own, and Peg returns, saying, "I only went in to go to the bathroom."

The following month I'm offered a job in San Francisco, recording the damage done to lives and property by the recent earthquake. Instead of going up to the cabin for a week with Gillian, I leave on short notice for California.

The night before, Carol and I have dinner in the City, and Gillian arrives unexpectedly. I'm seeing Carol on my last night because Gillian is tied up and can't get away. I haven't told Carol about Gillian, which Gillian realizes when Carol asks her how she knows me. Gillian answers that she met me through my mother, and manages to respond to all of Carol's questions without revealing her sexual orientation, that she and I are lovers, or even that we know one another well. When Carol leaves I tell Gillian I'm sorry.

"Are you living two lives?" she asks.

"Yes," I answer. "As your lover and as a recluse."

"A recluse from your best friend?"

"I told Carol I was seeing someone. I just didn't say who."

"How do you talk about me without saying my name, or do you call me Gil?"

"I haven't talked about you or us. I've wanted to, but every time I've seen Carol there have been others present. I was planning to tell her tonight."

"You could have seen her privately if you wanted to."

"I guess I didn't want to until now."

"Why?"

"I'm not sure."

"You seem very sure in bed."

"Carol intimidates me," I say. "She's aggressively curious."

"She's your best friend."

"No, you are. She's from another life, and I'm not sure I want to bring her into the new one. I'm not sure I want to share this with her. I think I want out of the friendship. That's why I've been reclusive. My old friends don't fit me any more."

"Then by all means tell her."

"I was going to, then run away to San Francisco. I warned you I'm a coward."

"You're inconsistent," Gillian says, looking a bit warmer than she has up to now.

"Gillian, I love you, and I don't mind anyone knowing that. But I do sometimes avoid confrontations. I challenged my Dad more than I challenged anyone and I avoided him much of the time. I know you don't admire me for that."

"I wish you had more confidence, but I won't bully you into it."

I reach out to Gillian and she says, "I should have called to say my plans changed."

"No, I loved the surprise."

Gillian and I kiss, and then she follows me into the darkroom where I pack my camera gear.

There's a photo of Mom pinned on my wall. Gillian looks at it. A minute later she says, "What do you think would have happened to us if she had lived?"

"I would have had to find someone else," I say.

"And I would have been jealous," Gillian says.

I look up at her. "You wouldn't have had any reason to be jealous. You would have had Mom."

Gillian gives me a look that says that isn't so, and I ask her, "Do you ever feel disloyal?"

"I know you better than I knew her, Bern. You have over-shadowed her. . . . Once or twice that has bothered me."

"I'll always be a little jealous that she was first," I say. "And I'll always wonder how you two were together, and hope you and I are better."

"I'm going to miss you these next weeks," Gillian says.

We shut off the lights in the apartment and go to bed. For a long while we don't make love. We touch arms and legs, clasp hands, kiss, then, face one another, staring into each other's eyes.

"I would never have traded Mom for you," I say finally. "I know you understand. We have that in common. Sometimes I think that's what makes your love so precious to me. Mom is like our lost child."

eleven

It is a clear
day in San Francisco,
and warmer than most places
in October, but an unusual gloom
hangs over the city because a neighborhood
has burned to the ground, and a catastrophe too pain-
ful to imagine, let alone view over and over again on television, has
taken place on the Bay Bridge and on an Oakland overpass.

I don't take pictures the day I arrive. I feel like a member of the
family, not a photographer. I talk to the people down at the Ma-
rina who lost their homes and who are not allowed to enter them
and rescue what little is left because it is too dangerous. The heartache and frustration and shock show on their faces. It will be there
for weeks, and I will photograph much of it.

During my second week in California I take a circuitous route
north across the San Rafael Bridge and south to Oakland. When
I arrive at the overpass I am at first so shocked by what I see I can
only sit in the car and stare. As I approach the scene, minutes later,
a worker comes up to me. He wants his picture taken. He wants the
world to see what has happened here. He would like everyone to
feel what he feels. I wish I were that good.

At the end of that day I am not relishing the thought of
bumper-to-bumper traffic back to San Francisco. I call Mark in Ber-

keley to ask him if I can stay overnight at his place. I would rather
he were not at home, that he were photographing in Africa or on
the ice cap, and I could let myself in with the extra key, but he is
at home.

I arrive weary from being on my feet all day and emotionally
drained from listening to family members tell me how and wonder
why their mother, father, sister, or spouse were on that overpass when
it collapsed. There is no way to relieve their horror and sorrow. With
rare exception they didn't mind having their pictures taken. No one
wanted to be on the nightly news, but most did hope their story
would be told in newspaper and magazine print.

Mark offers me a shower before dinner, and I accept. We eat
out on his patio. I talk about the last days and nothing else until
it is so dark that I can barely see Mark and he, me. Then, as Mom
did years ago in the dark up at the cabin, I tell Mark that I am in
love with a woman. I don't say Gillian was my mother's lover, or
that she is fifteen years my senior.

Mark asks me if I've had any trouble, and I answer, "No, I'm
in love. What trouble is that?"

"It's recent, then," he says.

"What do you mean?"

"I mean, it's new. You haven't had to face the difficulties yet."

"What difficulties?" I ask.

"Living in a straight world."

I'm silenced by my surprise. When I find my voice it's sharp.
"You've never let convention stand in your way."

"Are you pissed at me?" Mark asks.

"You *were* a friend."

"Hey, it's all right with me. I just think it will be tough."

"It's not all right with you. If I told you I was involved in anything else out of the mainstream, you'd be congratulating me."

"It isn't going to be easy, Bern."

"Oh, shut up, you know nothing about this."

"What caused the sea change?"

"You know something, Mark? I'm not going to tell you any more."

"Why is that?"

"Because you're jealous."

"What did you expect?"

"As always, too much," I say, and I get up, intending to leave. Mark stops me and tries to take me into his arms. "Jesus, you're arrogant," I say, pushing away from him.

On the road I decide I will call the airlines when I get back to the hotel and get on an earlier flight home. I'm glad I told Mark and glad he was a jerk. I didn't leave him this time feeling any ambivalence.

I have a short dialogue with Mom during the plane ride home the next day. I tell her that she was right to guess it would take someone else to get over Mark. Anxious to see that someone else, I rent a car at the airport and drive out to Shelter Island.

Janice's car is in the drive. I pull up behind it and park.

"Wonderful!" Gillian says when she sees me.

"Is it?" I ask, looking from her to Janice who is seated at the candlelit table with Gillian.

"Nothing's wrong, I hope," Gillian asks, getting up to kiss me.

"Hello, Janice. Fancy you being here."

"I thought you were coming back tomorrow," she says.

"Surprise!" I answer. "Have I interrupted something?"

"If you get yourself a plate you won't be interrupting anything," Gillian says.

"I'm not hungry," I answer, and I leave the dining room to go out to the car to get my bags. Gillian follows me out.

"Something is wrong," she says. "What is it?"

"That romantic dinner you're having," I say. "What were you two planning to do afterward, go to bed?"

"Bern, listen to yourself."

"Yeah, put it on me."

"Don't bother," Gillian says, referring to my bags. "I'll see you tomorrow after you've had some time to think over what you've just implied."

Gillian turns and starts back to the farmhouse. I get in the rental car and storm out of the drive.

After waiting half an hour in line at the ferry landing, I pull out of line and head back to the farmhouse. I don't see Janice, several cars behind me.

Gillian is washing dishes at the sink when I come in.

"What are you doing here?" she asks.

"I'm not some kid you can pack up and send off to her room to think over what she's done."

"Oh?"

"And if I had toddled off to New York you wouldn't be the slightest bit interested in me."

"Oh?" Gillian says again.

"You don't really want the upper hand, do you?"

Gillian looks at me pointblank and says nothing.

"I wanted to find you at home alone, pining for me," I say.

"Are you sure you want that?"

I take off my jacket and sit down at the kitchen table. I'm exhausted from the ordeal of California, the long flight home, and the drive here. I lay my head down and say, "I'm sorry. I know I was rude."

Gillian wipes her hands dry and comes over to me. "Your rudeness hurt less than your accusation."

"I'm sorry about that, too," I say. "But it's not like Janice wouldn't like to go to bed with you."

"It takes two to tango."

"Why have a candlelight dinner with someone you're not interested in?" I ask.

"I like to eat by candlelight."

"I wish you'd eaten in here with the ceiling light on," I say, smiling for the first time. Gillian bends down to put an arm around me.

"I have been pining away for you," she says.

I stand up so we can embrace and start to cry.

"Something has happened," Gillian says concerned. "Shall we talk about it?"

"No. I want to go to bed."

Minutes later, naked in bed beside Gillian, I ask where Janice is. "She's not in the guest room next door, is she?"

Gillian climbs on top of me and says, "You're such a fool."

"Oh, that's right, her car was gone. Unless she parked it out of sight. She's not hiding in the closet, is she?"

"I wish you'd get her off your mind," Gillian says, before kissing my neck and shoulder.

"I missed you," I say.

"What did you miss most?"

"This, your body against mine. I was lonely in bed and didn't sleep well. I came back early so I could get a good night's sleep."

"Is that what you want?" Gillian says touching me.

Her cool hand feels wonderful. I have been yearning for this. Her touch is intoxicating. I let go of my concerns and inhibitions and enjoy the frenzied feeling at my center. I want her on me and in me, now and forever. I want to live every minute of my life like this. I don't want her loving to stop, but I don't want to stop what's building in me, either.

I don't exactly know where this passion comes from in me, why I respond to this woman as I never have to anyone else. It is true that throughout my life I have watched women more than men. I wanted someone like my mother and thought it was her personality, not her gender, that I was drawn to. I sought the affection of men to fulfill my desire for love, and I was not always disappointed. But no one ever felt like this. This is not strange, only surprising. And love is always surprising. I feel the inherent goodness in our love and know it is the kind of love families were meant to spring from. It does not matter that we are both women.

In the morning Gillian and I linger in bed, catching up with one another.

"What do you think of my soft elbows?" Gillian asks out of the blue.

"Soft elbows?" I repeat because I'm not sure I've heard her correctly.

"And the gray in my hair, and the lines on my face and hands?"

"Nothing about you is unappealing," I say, surprised by this questioning. "I didn't know you worried about those things," I say.

"I was looking at myself yesterday, wondering how you see me. I don't think about myself aging, until I see it. I'm getting old, Bern."

"So am I," I say. "And on me it doesn't look as good."

"If we cut our ties and moved some place new to both of us, would you be happier?" Gillian asks.

"What is it, Gillian? This isn't like you."

"Would you be happier?"

"I've thought about it," I say. "But you're settled here, and I need to be close to the City."

"Would you like to go away for a few months? Away from friends, some place where no one knows us, where we'll be seen as a couple?"

"That would be nice."

"Could you? Get away?"

"Where did you have in mind?"

"The French countryside."

Gillian and I go to France during February and March of that year. Much of February is wet and cold, but we don't mind walking under an umbrella together, slipping into cafes to warm ourselves, and going to bed early.

We return to the States at the end of March. Gillian to her gardens, me to Old Field. I have a buyer for the house. For two weeks Meg and I sort and pack.

twelve

The awnings
aren't up yet, but the
grass is turning green again
and purple crocuses line the front flower
bed. A van is parked in the drive, loaded with
furniture, books, odds and ends. Inside the house, Gillian
is vacuuming the library where two hours ago boxes and furniture
were waiting to be loaded into the truck outside.

Some of the rooms in the house have furniture. All have their
curtains. The new owner bought a third of the contents. Another
third went to an auction house, and what wasn't given away from
the rest is now in the van outside. Jeff's desk is there, and so is Mom's
reading chair and ottoman, and my bed.

I'm upstairs, standing in the rectangle of carpet that was once
hidden by my bed, when I hear Jeff.

*In the next instant Jeff leaps on my bed, on top of me, and we wres-
tle to the floor.*

"Come see it, Bern."

"What happened to your face?" I ask.

*"It's just paint. Come see it." Jeff gets up off the floor. "Aren't you
even a little curious?"*

Jeff has been doing something secretive in his room for weeks. No one has been able to guess correctly what that is.

"Am I the first?" I ask, getting out of a tangle of sheets.

"If you hurry," he says, and he runs from my room to his.

Painted on the ceiling of Jeff's room, with paint that glows in the dark, is the solar system.

Nothing is left in Jeff's room except the solar system on the ceiling and the curtains at the window. I close the door. In the hall I hear someone else call out to me.

Mom is in the sewing room, putting the hem in my prom dress, although I have no date for the dance. The boy I was going to go with got sick the day before.

"It's all set," she says.

"I told you not to do it."

"Why can't your dad take you to the prom?"

"Mom, get serious."

"I am."

"It's all right, Mom. I'm glad he got sick. I hate those silly dances."

"Really, Bern?"

"Really, Mom. I'd rather go to a movie."

"Would you take me with you?"

"Sure, but I'm not wearing the dress."

Mom holds out the dress on its hanger for me and says, "You never know, someday you might decide to wear it."

Instead of taking the dress, I bend down and pick up Mom's round sewing basket.

In the hallway I run into Dad. "We're going now," he says.

"Mom, too?" I ask.

"Yes. Are you sure you don't want to?"

"When are you coming back?"

"One of us will be home tonight."

I go to my room to get my camera. I want to take a picture of my brother before he leaves for the hospital. I don't tell Dad or admit to myself that I'm afraid I'll never see Jeff again, that I don't want to go with them because I don't want to see the end. But I can't let go without taking a photo of him.

I'm crying when I pass Gillian on the stairs.

"Didn't you hear me?" she asks. "I've been calling you."

We stand together for a brief moment before I start down the next step with her.

At the bottom I give Gillian Mom's sewing basket to take out to the van, then walk into the library. So much life took place in this house it is difficult to step away from it.

I feel as I did the day I left home for college. Although I only went a few miles into the City, and I am now only going a few miles out to Shelter Island, I knew when I returned nothing would be the same. I took a dozen pictures on my way out.

As I hop into the van Gillian says, "Let's hope the rain holds off."

"Where's the basket?" I ask.

"In the back with the rest."

"I didn't take any pictures."

"Did that surprise you?" she asks.

"Yes, sort of."

Gillian starts up the motor, and we pull away from Old Field on a spring day that promises rain. I would have taken pictures if it weren't for her. It's easier to let go with Gillian beside me.

Other titles from Firebrand Books include:

Artemis In Echo Park, Poetry by Eloise Klein Healy/$8.95

Beneath My Heart, Poetry by Janice Gould/$8.95

The Big Mama Stories by Shay Youngblood/$8.95

The Black Back-Ups, Poetry by Kate Rushin/$8.95

A Burst Of Light, Essays by Audre Lorde/$8.95

Cecile, Stories by Ruthann Robson/$8.95

Crime Against Nature, Poetry by Minnie Bruce Pratt/$8.95

Diamonds Are A Dyke's Best Friend by Yvonne Zipter/$9.95

Dykes To Watch Out For, Cartoons by Alison Bechdel/$7.95

Dykes To Watch Out For: The Sequel, Cartoons by Alison Bechdel/$8.95

Exile In The Promised Land, A Memoir by Marcia Freedman/$8.95

Experimental Love, Poetry by Cheryl Clarke/$8.95

Eye Of A Hurricane, Stories by Ruthann Robson/$8.95

The Fires Of Bride, A Novel by Ellen Galford/$8.95

Food & Spirits, Stories by Beth Brant (*Degonwadonti*)/$8.95

Forty-Three Septembers, Essays by Jewelle Gomez/$10.95

Free Ride, A Novel by Marilyn Gayle/$9.95

A Gathering Of Spirit, A Collection by North American Indian Women edited by Beth Brant (*Degonwadonti*)/$10.95

Getting Home Alive by Aurora Levins Morales and Rosario Morales/$9.95

The Gilda Stories, A Novel by Jewelle Gomez/$9.95

Good Enough To Eat, A Novel by Lesléa Newman/$8.95

Humid Pitch, Narrative Poetry by Cheryl Clarke/$8.95

Jewish Women's Call For Peace edited by Rita Falbel, Irena Klepfisz, and Donna Nevel/$4.95

Jonestown & Other Madness, Poetry by Pat Parker/$7.95

Just Say Yes, A Novel by Judith McDaniel/$9.95

The Land Of Look Behind, Prose and Poetry by Michelle Cliff/$8.95

Legal Tender, A Mystery by Marion Foster/$9.95

Lesbian (Out)law, Survival Under the Rule of Law by Ruthann Robson/$9.95

A Letter To Harvey Milk, Short Stories by Lesléa Newman/$8.95

Letting In The Night, A Novel by Joan Lindau/$8.95

Living As A Lesbian, Poetry by Cheryl Clarke/$7.95

Metamorphosis, Reflections On Recovery by Judith McDaniel/$7.95

Mohawk Trail by Beth Brant (*Degonwadonti*)/$7.95

Moll Cutpurse, A Novel by Ellen Galford/$7.95

The Monarchs Are Flying, A Novel by Marion Foster/$8.95

More Dykes To Watch Out For, Cartoons by Alison Bechdel/$7.95

Movement In Black, Poetry by Pat Parker/$8.95

My Mama's Dead Squirrel, Lesbian Essays on Southern Culture by Mab Segrest/$9.95

New, Improved! Dykes To Watch Out For, Cartoons by Alison Bechdel/$7.95

The Other Sappho, A Novel by Ellen Frye/$8.95

Out In The World, International Lesbian Organizing by Shelley Anderson/$4.95

Politics Of The Heart, A Lesbian Parenting Anthology edited by Sandra Pollack and Jeanne Vaughn/$12.95

Presenting. . . Sister NoBlues by Hattie Gossett/$8.95

Rebellion, Essays 1980-1991 by Minnie Bruce Pratt/$10.95

Restoring The Color Of Roses by Barrie Jean Borich/$9.95

A Restricted Country by Joan Nestle/$9.95

Running Fiercely Toward A High Thin Sound, A Novel by Judith Katz/$9.95

Sacred Space by Geraldine Hatch Hanon/$9.95

Sanctuary, A Journey by Judith McDaniel/$7.95

Sans Souci, And Other Stories by Dionne Brand/$8.95

Scuttlebutt, A Novel by Jana Williams/$8.95

Shoulders, A Novel by Georgia Cotrell/$8.95

Simple Songs, Stories by Vickie Sears/$8.95

Spawn Of Dykes To Watch Out For, Cartoons by Alison Bechdel/$8.95

Speaking Dreams, Science Fiction by Severna Park/$9.95

Stone Butch Blues, A Novel by Leslie Feinberg/$10.95

The Sun Is Not Merciful, Short Stories by Anna Lee Walters/$8.95

Talking Indian, Reflections on Survival and Writing by Anna Lee Walters/$10.95

Tender Warriors, A Novel by Rachel Guido deVries/$8.95

This Is About Incest by Margaret Randall/$8.95

The Threshing Floor, Short Stories by Barbara Burford/$7.95

Trash, Stories by Dorothy Allison/$9.95

We Say We Love Each Other, Poetry by Minnie Bruce Pratt/$8.95

The Women Who Hate Me, Poetry by Dorothy Allison/$8.95

Words To The Wise, A Writer's Guide to Feminist and Lesbian Periodicals & Publishers by Andrea Fleck Clardy/$5.95

The Worry Girl, Stories from a Childhood by Andrea Freud Loewenstein/$8.95

Yours In Struggle, Three Feminist Perspectives on Anti-Semitism and Racism by Elly Bulkin, Minnie Bruce Pratt, and Barbara Smith/$8.95

You can buy Firebrand titles at your bookstore, or order them directly from the publisher (141 The Commons, Ithaca, New York 14850, 607-272-0000).

Please include $2.00 shipping for the first book and $.50 for each additional book.

A free catalog is available on request.